The Three Theban Plays

Antigone - Oedipus the King - Oedipus at Colonus

By Sophocles

Translated by F. Storr

Published in 2018

Logo art adapted from work by Bernard Gagnon

ISBN-13: 978-1-387-81645-3

This translation was first published in 1912 by Harvard University Press and William
Heinemann Ltd, London

Contents

Oedipus the King

Argument

To Laius, King of Thebes, an oracle foretold that the child born to him by his queen Jocasta would slay his father and wed his mother. So when in time a son was born the infant's feet were riveted together and he was left to die on Mount Cithaeron. But a shepherd found the babe and tended him, and delivered him to another shepherd who took him to his master, the King of Corinth. Polybus being childless adopted the boy, who grew up believing that he was indeed the King's son. Afterwards doubting his parentage he inquired of the Delphic god and heard himself the word declared before to Laius. Wherefore he fled from what he deemed his father's house and in his flight he encountered and unwillingly slew his father Laius. Arriving at Thebes he answered the riddle of the Sphinx and the grateful Thebans made their deliverer king. So he reigned in the room of Laius, and espoused the widowed queen. Children were born to them and Thebes prospered under his rule, but again a grievous plague fell upon the city. Again the oracle was consulted and it bade them purge themselves of blood-guiltiness. Oedipus denounces the crime of which he is unaware, and undertakes to track out the criminal. Step by step it is brought home to him that he is the man. The closing scene reveals Jocasta slain by her own hand and Oedipus blinded by his own act and praying for death or exile.

Dramatis Personae

Oedipus.
The Priest of Zeus.
Creon.
Chorus of Theban Elders.
Teiresias.
Jocasta.
Messenger.
Herd of Laius.
Second Messenger.

Scene: Thebes. Before the Palace of Oedipus. Suppliants of all ages are seated round the altar at the palace doors, at their head a PRIEST OF ZEUS. To them enter OEDIPUS.

OEDIPUS
My children, latest born to Cadmus old,
Why sit ye here as suppliants, in your hands
Branches of olive filleted with wool?
What means this reek of incense everywhere,
And everywhere laments and litanies?
Children, it were not meet that I should learn
From others, and am hither come, myself,
I Oedipus, your world-renowned king.
Ho! aged sire, whose venerable locks
Proclaim thee spokesman of this company,
Explain your mood and purport. Is it dread
Of ill that moves you or a boon ye crave?
My zeal in your behalf ye cannot doubt;
Ruthless indeed were I and obdurate
If such petitioners as you I spurned.

PRIEST
Yea, Oedipus, my sovereign lord and king,
Thou seest how both extremes of age besiege
Thy palace altars—fledglings hardly winged,
and greybeards bowed with years; priests, as am I
of Zeus, and these the flower of our youth.
Meanwhile, the common folk, with wreathed boughs
Crowd our two market-places, or before
Both shrines of Pallas congregate, or where
Ismenus gives his oracles by fire.
For, as thou seest thyself, our ship of State,
Sore buffeted, can no more lift her head,
Foundered beneath a weltering surge of blood.
A blight is on our harvest in the ear,
A blight upon the grazing flocks and herds,
A blight on wives in travail; and withal
Armed with his blazing torch the God of Plague

5

Hath swooped upon our city emptying
The house of Cadmus, and the murky realm
Of Pluto is full fed with groans and tears.
  Therefore, O King, here at thy hearth we sit,
I and these children; not as deeming thee
A new divinity, but the first of men;
First in the common accidents of life,
And first in visitations of the Gods.
Art thou not he who coming to the town
of Cadmus freed us from the tax we paid
To the fell songstress? Nor hadst thou received
Prompting from us or been by others schooled;
No, by a god inspired (so all men deem,
And testify) didst thou renew our life.
And now, O Oedipus, our peerless king,
All we thy votaries beseech thee, find
Some succor, whether by a voice from heaven
Whispered, or haply known by human wit.
Tried counselors, methinks, are aptest found 1
To furnish for the future pregnant rede.
Upraise, O chief of men, upraise our State!
Look to thy laurels! for thy zeal of yore
Our country's savior thou art justly hailed:
O never may we thus record thy reign:—
"He raised us up only to cast us down."
Uplift us, build our city on a rock.
Thy happy star ascendant brought us luck,
O let it not decline! If thou wouldst rule
This land, as now thou reignest, better sure
To rule a peopled than a desert realm.
Nor battlements nor galleys aught avail,
If men to man and guards to guard them tail.

OEDIPUS
Ah! my poor children, known, ah, known too well,
The quest that brings you hither and your need.
Ye sicken all, well wot I, yet my pain,
How great soever yours, outtops it all.
Your sorrow touches each man severally,
Him and none other, but I grieve at once
Both for the general and myself and you.
Therefore ye rouse no sluggard from day-dreams.
Many, my children, are the tears I've wept,
And threaded many a maze of weary thought.
Thus pondering one clue of hope I caught,
And tracked it up; I have sent Menoeceus' son,
Creon, my consort's brother, to inquire
Of Pythian Phoebus at his Delphic shrine,
How I might save the State by act or word.
And now I reckon up the tale of days
Since he set forth, and marvel how he fares.
'Tis strange, this endless tarrying, passing strange.
But when he comes, then I were base indeed,
If I perform not all the god declares.
PRIEST
Thy words are well timed; even as thou speakest
That shouting tells me Creon is at hand.
OEDIPUS
O King Apollo! may his joyous looks
Be presage of the joyous news he brings!
PRIEST
As I surmise, 'tis welcome; else his head
Had scarce been crowned with berry-laden bays.

OEDIPUS
We soon shall know; he's now in earshot range.
[Enter CREON]
My royal cousin, say, Menoeceus' child,
What message hast thou brought us from the god?
CREON
Good news, for e'en intolerable ills,
Finding right issue, tend to naught but good.
OEDIPUS
How runs the oracle? thus far thy words
Give me no ground for confidence or fear.
CREON
If thou wouldst hear my message publicly,
I'll tell thee straight, or with thee pass within.
OEDIPUS
Speak before all; the burden that I bear
Is more for these my subjects than myself.
CREON
Let me report then all the god declared.
King Phoebus bids us straitly extirpate
A fell pollution that infests the land,
And no more harbor an inveterate sore.
OEDIPUS
What expiation means he? What's amiss?
CREON
Banishment, or the shedding blood for blood.
This stain of blood makes shipwreck of our state.
OEDIPUS
Whom can he mean, the miscreant thus denounced?
CREON
Before thou didst assume the helm of State,
The sovereign of this land was Laius.

OEDIPUS
I heard as much, but never saw the man.
CREON
He fell; and now the god's command is plain:
Punish his takers-off, whoe'er they be.
OEDIPUS
Where are they? Where in the wide world to find
The far, faint traces of a bygone crime?
CREON
In this land, said the god; "who seeks shall find;
Who sits with folded hands or sleeps is blind."
OEDIPUS
Was he within his palace, or afield,
Or traveling, when Laius met his fate?
CREON
Abroad; he started, so he told us, bound
For Delphi, but he never thence returned.
OEDIPUS
Came there no news, no fellow-traveler
To give some clue that might be followed up?
CREON
But one escape, who flying for dear life,
Could tell of all he saw but one thing sure.
OEDIPUS
And what was that? One clue might lead us far,
With but a spark of hope to guide our quest.
CREON
Robbers, he told us, not one bandit but
A troop of knaves, attacked and murdered him.
OEDIPUS
Did any bandit dare so bold a stroke,
Unless indeed he were suborned from Thebes?

CREON

So 'twas surmised, but none was found to avenge
His murder mid the trouble that ensued.

OEDIPUS

What trouble can have hindered a full quest,
When royalty had fallen thus miserably?

CREON

The riddling Sphinx compelled us to let slide
The dim past and attend to instant needs.

OEDIPUS

Well, I will start afresh and once again
Make dark things clear. Right worthy the concern
Of Phoebus, worthy thine too, for the dead;
I also, as is meet, will lend my aid
To avenge this wrong to Thebes and to the god.
Not for some far-off kinsman, but myself,
Shall I expel this poison in the blood;
For whoso slew that king might have a mind
To strike me too with his assassin hand.
Therefore in righting him I serve myself.
Up, children, haste ye, quit these altar stairs,
Take hence your suppliant wands, go summon hither
The Theban commons. With the god's good help
Success is sure; 'tis ruin if we fail.

[Exeunt OEDIPUS and CREON]

PRIEST

Come, children, let us hence; these gracious words
Forestall the very purpose of our suit.
And may the god who sent this oracle
Save us withal and rid us of this pest.

[Exeunt PRIEST and SUPPLIANTS]

CHORUS

(Str. 1)

Sweet-voiced daughter of Zeus from thy gold-paved Pythian shrine
  Wafted to Thebes divine,
What dost thou bring me? My soul is racked and shivers with fear.
  (Healer of Delos, hear!)
Hast thou some pain unknown before,
Or with the circling years renewest a penance of yore?
Offspring of golden Hope, thou voice immortal, O tell me.

(Ant. 1)

First on Athene I call; O Zeus-born goddess, defend!
  Goddess and sister, befriend,
Artemis, Lady of Thebes, high-throned in the midst of our mart!
  Lord of the death-winged dart!
  Your threefold aid I crave
 From death and ruin our city to save.
If in the days of old when we nigh had perished, ye drave
From our land the fiery plague, be near us now and defend us!

(Str. 2)

 Ah me, what countless woes are mine!
 All our host is in decline;
 Weaponless my spirit lies.
 Earth her gracious fruits denies;
 Women wail in barren throes;
 Life on life downstriken goes,
 Swifter than the wind bird's flight,
 Swifter than the Fire-God's might,
 To the westering shores of Night.

(Ant. 2)

 Wasted thus by death on death
 All our city perisheth.
 Corpses spread infection round;
 None to tend or mourn is found.
 Wailing on the altar stair
 Wives and grandams rend the air—
 Long-drawn moans and piercing cries
 Blent with prayers and litanies.
 Golden child of Zeus, O hear
 Let thine angel face appear!

(Str. 3)
And grant that Ares whose hot breath I
feel,
    Though without targe or steel
He stalks, whose voice is as the battle
shout,
May turn in sudden rout,
To the unharbored Thracian waters
sped,
    Or Amphitrite's bed.
    For what night leaves undone,
    Smit by the morrow's sun
Perisheth. Father Zeus, whose hand
Doth wield the lightning brand,
Slay him beneath thy levin bold, we pray,
    Slay him, O slay!

(Ant. 3)
O that thine arrows too, Lycean King,
    From that taut bow's gold string,
Might fly abroad, the champions of our
rights;
    Yea, and the flashing lights
Of Artemis, wherewith the huntress
sweeps
    Across the Lycian steeps.
Thee too I call with golden-snooded hair,
    Whose name our land doth bear,
Bacchus to whom thy Maenads Evoe
shout;
    Come with thy bright torch, rout,
    Blithe god whom we adore,
    The god whom gods abhor.

[Enter OEDIPUS.]

OEDIPUS
Ye pray; 'tis well, but would ye hear my
words
And heed them and apply the remedy,
Ye might perchance find comfort and
relief.
Mind you, I speak as one who comes a
stranger
To this report, no less than to the crime;
For how unaided could I track it far
Without a clue? Which lacking (for too
late
Was I enrolled a citizen of Thebes)
This proclamation I address to all:—
Thebans, if any knows the man by whom
Laius, son of Labdacus, was slain,
I summon him to make clean shrift to
me.
And if he shrinks, let him reflect that
thus
Confessing he shall 'scape the capital
charge;
For the worst penalty that shall befall
him
Is banishment—unscathed he shall
depart.
But if an alien from a foreign land
Be known to any as the murderer,
Let him who knows speak out, and he
shall have
Due recompense from me and thanks to
boot.
But if ye still keep silence, if through fear
For self or friends ye disregard my hest,
Hear what I then resolve; I lay my ban
On the assassin whosoe'er he be.
Let no man in this land, whereof I hold
The sovereign rule, harbor or speak to
him;
Give him no part in prayer or sacrifice
Or lustral rites, but hound him from your
homes.
For this is our defilement, so the god
Hath lately shown to me by oracles.
Thus as their champion I maintain the
cause
Both of the god and of the murdered
King.
And on the murderer this curse I lay
(On him and all the partners in his
guilt):—
Wretch, may he pine in utter
wretchedness!
And for myself, if with my privity
He gain admittance to my hearth, I pray
The curse I laid on others fall on me.
See that ye give effect to all my hest,

9

For my sake and the god's and for our land,
A desert blasted by the wrath of heaven.
For, let alone the god's express command,
It were a scandal ye should leave unpurged
The murder of a great man and your king,
Nor track it home. And now that I am lord,
Successor to his throne, his bed, his wife,
(And had he not been frustrate in the hope
Of issue, common children of one womb
Had forced a closer bond twixt him and me,
But Fate swooped down upon him), therefore I
His blood-avenger will maintain his cause
As though he were my sire, and leave no stone
Unturned to track the assassin or avenge
The son of Labdacus, of Polydore,
Of Cadmus, and Agenor first of the race.
And for the disobedient thus I pray:
May the gods send them neither timely fruits
Of earth, nor teeming increase of the womb,
But may they waste and pine, as now they waste,
Aye and worse stricken; but to all of you,
My loyal subjects who approve my acts,
May Justice, our ally, and all the gods
Be gracious and attend you evermore.

CHORUS
The oath thou profferest, sire, I take and swear.
I slew him not myself, nor can I name
The slayer. For the quest, 'twere well, methinks
That Phoebus, who proposed the riddle, himself

Should give the answer—who the murderer was.

OEDIPUS
Well argued; but no living man can hope
To force the gods to speak against their will.

CHORUS
May I then say what seems next best to me?

OEDIPUS
Aye, if there be a third best, tell it too.

CHORUS
My liege, if any man sees eye to eye
With our lord Phoebus, 'tis our prophet, lord
Teiresias; he of all men best might guide
A searcher of this matter to the light.

OEDIPUS
Here too my zeal has nothing lagged, for twice
At Creon's instance have I sent to fetch him,
And long I marvel why he is not here.

CHORUS
I mind me too of rumors long ago—
Mere gossip.

OEDIPUS
          Tell them, I would fain know all.

CHORUS
'Twas said he fell by travelers.

OEDIPUS
                    So I heard,
But none has seen the man who saw him fall.

CHORUS
Well, if he knows what fear is, he will quail
And flee before the terror of thy curse.

OEDIPUS
Words scare not him who blenches not at deeds.

CHORUS
But here is one to arraign him. Lo, at length

They bring the god-inspired seer in whom
Above all other men is truth inborn.
[Enter TEIRESIAS, led by a boy.]

OEDIPUS
Teiresias, seer who comprehendest all,
Lore of the wise and hidden mysteries,
High things of heaven and low things of the earth,
Thou knowest, though thy blinded eyes see naught,
What plague infects our city; and we turn
To thee, O seer, our one defense and shield.
The purport of the answer that the God
Returned to us who sought his oracle,
The messengers have doubtless told thee—how
One course alone could rid us of the pest,
To find the murderers of Laius,
And slay them or expel them from the land.
Therefore begrudging neither augury
Nor other divination that is thine,
O save thyself, thy country, and thy king,
Save all from this defilement of blood shed.
On thee we rest. This is man's highest end,
To others' service all his powers to lend.

TEIRESIAS
Alas, alas, what misery to be wise
When wisdom profits nothing! This old lore
I had forgotten; else I were not here.

OEDIPUS
What ails thee? Why this melancholy mood?

TEIRESIAS
Let me go home; prevent me not; 'twere best
That thou shouldst bear thy burden and I mine.

OEDIPUS

For shame! no true-born Theban patriot
Would thus withhold the word of prophecy.

TEIRESIAS
Thy words, O king, are wide of the mark, and I
For fear lest I too trip like thee...

OEDIPUS
                              Oh speak,
Withhold not, I adjure thee, if thou know'st,
Thy knowledge. We are all thy suppliants.

TEIRESIAS
Aye, for ye all are witless, but my voice
Will ne'er reveal my miseries—or thine.

2

OEDIPUS
What then, thou knowest, and yet willst not speak!
Wouldst thou betray us and destroy the State?

TEIRESIAS
I will not vex myself nor thee. Why ask
Thus idly what from me thou shalt not learn?

OEDIPUS
Monster! thy silence would incense a flint.
Will nothing loose thy tongue? Can nothing melt thee,
Or shake thy dogged taciturnity?

TEIRESIAS
Thou blam'st my mood and seest not thine own
Wherewith thou art mated; no, thou taxest me.

OEDIPUS
And who could stay his choler when he heard
How insolently thou dost flout the State?

TEIRESIAS
Well, it will come what will, though I be mute.

OEDIPUS

Since come it must, thy duty is to tell me.
TEIRESIAS
I have no more to say; storm as thou willst,
And give the rein to all thy pent-up rage.
OEDIPUS
Yea, I am wroth, and will not stint my words,
But speak my whole mind. Thou methinks thou art he,
Who planned the crime, aye, and performed it too,
All save the assassination; and if thou
Hadst not been blind, I had been sworn to boot
That thou alone didst do the bloody deed.
TEIRESIAS
Is it so? Then I charge thee to abide
By thine own proclamation; from this day
Speak not to these or me. Thou art the man,
Thou the accursed polluter of this land.
OEDIPUS
Vile slanderer, thou blurtest forth these taunts,
And think'st forsooth as seer to go scot free.
TEIRESIAS
Yea, I am free, strong in the strength of truth.
OEDIPUS
Who was thy teacher? not methinks thy art.
TEIRESIAS
Thou, goading me against my will to speak.
OEDIPUS
What speech? repeat it and resolve my doubt.
TEIRESIAS
Didst miss my sense wouldst thou goad me on?
OEDIPUS

I but half caught thy meaning; say it again.
TEIRESIAS
I say thou art the murderer of the man
Whose murderer thou pursuest.
OEDIPUS
                    Thou shalt rue it
Twice to repeat so gross a calumny.
TEIRESIAS
Must I say more to aggravate thy rage?
OEDIPUS
Say all thou wilt; it will be but waste of breath.
TEIRESIAS
I say thou livest with thy nearest kin
In infamy, unwitting in thy shame.
OEDIPUS
Think'st thou for aye unscathed to wag thy tongue?
TEIRESIAS
Yea, if the might of truth can aught prevail.
OEDIPUS
With other men, but not with thee, for thou
In ear, wit, eye, in everything art blind.
TEIRESIAS
Poor fool to utter gibes at me which all
Here present will cast back on thee ere long.
OEDIPUS
Offspring of endless Night, thou hast no power
O'er me or any man who sees the sun.
TEIRESIAS
No, for thy weird is not to fall by me.
I leave to Apollo what concerns the god.
OEDIPUS
Is this a plot of Creon, or thine own?
TEIRESIAS
Not Creon, thou thyself art thine own bane.
OEDIPUS
O wealth and empiry and skill by skill
Outwitted in the battlefield of life,

12

What spite and envy follow in your train!
See, for this crown the State conferred
on me.
A gift, a thing I sought not, for this crown
The trusty Creon, my familiar friend,
Hath lain in wait to oust me and
suborned
This mountebank, this juggling
charlatan,
This tricksy beggar-priest, for gain alone
Keen-eyed, but in his proper art stone-
blind.
Say, sirrah, hast thou ever proved thyself
A prophet? When the riddling Sphinx
was here
Why hadst thou no deliverance for this
folk?
And yet the riddle was not to be solved
By guess-work but required the
prophet's art;
Wherein thou wast found lacking;
neither birds
Nor sign from heaven helped thee, but I
came,
The simple Oedipus; I stopped her
mouth
By mother wit, untaught of auguries.
This is the man whom thou wouldst
undermine,
In hope to reign with Creon in my stead.
Methinks that thou and thine abettor
soon
Will rue your plot to drive the scapegoat
out.
Thank thy grey hairs that thou hast still
to learn
What chastisement such arrogance
deserves.

CHORUS
To us it seems that both the seer and
thou,
O Oedipus, have spoken angry words.
This is no time to wrangle but consult
How best we may fulfill the oracle.

TEIRESIAS
King as thou art, free speech at least is
mine
To make reply; in this I am thy peer.
I own no lord but Loxias; him I serve
And ne'er can stand enrolled as Creon's
man.
Thus then I answer: since thou hast not
spared
To twit me with my blindness—thou
hast eyes,
Yet see'st not in what misery thou art
fallen,
Nor where thou dwellest nor with whom
for mate.
Dost know thy lineage? Nay, thou
know'st it not,
And all unwitting art a double foe
To thine own kin, the living and the
dead;
Aye and the dogging curse of mother and
sire
One day shall drive thee, like a two-
edged sword,
Beyond our borders, and the eyes that
now
See clear shall henceforward endless
night.
Ah whither shall thy bitter cry not reach,
What crag in all Cithaeron but shall then
Reverberate thy wail, when thou hast
found
With what a hymeneal thou wast borne
Home, but to no fair haven, on the gale!
Aye, and a flood of ills thou guessest not
Shall set thyself and children in one line.
Flout then both Creon and my words, for
none
Of mortals shall be striken worse than
thou.

OEDIPUS
Must I endure this fellow's insolence?
A murrain on thee! Get thee hence!
Begone
Avaunt! and never cross my threshold
more.

TEIRESIAS

I ne'er had come hadst thou not bidden me.

OEDIPUS

I know not thou wouldst utter folly, else
Long hadst thou waited to be summoned here.

TEIRESIAS

Such am I—as it seems to thee a fool,
But to the parents who begat thee, wise.

OEDIPUS

What sayest thou—"parents"? Who begat me, speak?

TEIRESIAS

This day shall be thy birth-day, and thy grave.

OEDIPUS

Thou lov'st to speak in riddles and dark words.

TEIRESIAS

In reading riddles who so skilled as thou?

OEDIPUS

Twit me with that wherein my greatness lies.

TEIRESIAS

And yet this very greatness proved thy bane.

OEDIPUS

No matter if I saved the commonwealth.

TEIRESIAS

'Tis time I left thee. Come, boy, take me home.

OEDIPUS

Aye, take him quickly, for his presence irks
And lets me; gone, thou canst not plague me more.

TEIRESIAS

I go, but first will tell thee why I came.
Thy frown I dread not, for thou canst not harm me.
Hear then: this man whom thou hast sought to arrest
With threats and warrants this long while, the wretch
Who murdered Laius—that man is here.
He passes for an alien in the land
But soon shall prove a Theban, native born.
And yet his fortune brings him little joy;
For blind of seeing, clad in beggar's weeds,
For purple robes, and leaning on his staff,
To a strange land he soon shall grope his way.
And of the children, inmates of his home,
He shall be proved the brother and the sire,
Of her who bare him son and husband both,
Co-partner, and assassin of his sire.
Go in and ponder this, and if thou find
That I have missed the mark, henceforth declare
I have no wit nor skill in prophecy.
[Exeunt TEIRESIAS and OEDIPUS]

CHORUS

(Str. 1)
Who is he by voice immortal named from Pythia's rocky cell,
Doer of foul deeds of bloodshed, horrors that no tongue can tell?
A foot for flight he needs
Fleeter than storm-swift steeds,
For on his heels doth follow,
Armed with the lightnings of his Sire, Apollo.
Like sleuth-hounds too
The Fates pursue.

(Ant. 1)
Yea, but now flashed forth the summons from Parnassus' snowy peak,
"Near and far the undiscovered doer of this murder seek!"
Now like a sullen bull he roves
Through forest brakes and upland groves,

14

And vainly seeks to fly
The doom that ever nigh
Flits o'er his head,
Still by the avenging Phoebus sped,
The voice divine,
From Earth's mid shrine.
(Str. 2)
Sore perplexed am I by the words of the master seer.
Are they true, are they false? I know not and bridle my tongue for
 fear,
Fluttered with vague surmise; nor present nor future is clear.
Quarrel of ancient date or in days still near know I none
Twixt the Labdacidan house and our ruler, Polybus' son.
Proof is there none: how then can I challenge our King's good name,
How in a blood-feud join for an untracked deed of shame?
(Ant. 2)
All wise are Zeus and Apollo, and nothing is hid from their ken;
They are gods; and in wits a man may surpass his fellow men;
But that a mortal seer knows more than I know—where
Hath this been proven? Or how without sign assured, can I blame
Him who saved our State when the winged songstress came,
Tested and tried in the light of us all, like gold assayed?
How can I now assent when a crime is on Oedipus laid?
CREON
Friends, countrymen, I learn King Oedipus
Hath laid against me a most grievous charge,
And come to you protesting. If he deems
That I have harmed or injured him in aught

By word or deed in this our present trouble,
I care not to prolong the span of life,
Thus ill-reputed; for the calumny
Hits not a single blot, but blasts my name,
If by the general voice I am denounced
False to the State and false by you my friends.
CHORUS
This taunt, it well may be, was blurted out
In petulance, not spoken advisedly.
CREON
Did any dare pretend that it was I
Prompted the seer to utter a forged charge?
CHORUS
Such things were said; with what intent I know not.
CREON
Were not his wits and vision all astray
When upon me he fixed this monstrous charge?
CHORUS
I know not; to my sovereign's acts I am blind.
But lo, he comes to answer for himself.
[Enter OEDIPUS.]
OEDIPUS
Sirrah, what mak'st thou here? Dost thou presume
To approach my doors, thou brazen-faced rogue,
My murderer and the filcher of my crown?
Come, answer this, didst thou detect in me
Some touch of cowardice or witlessness,
That made thee undertake this enterprise?
I seemed forsooth too simple to perceive
The serpent stealing on me in the dark,
Or else too weak to scotch it when I saw.
This thou art witless seeking to possess

Without a following or friends the crown,
A prize that followers and wealth must win.
CREON
Attend me. Thou hast spoken, 'tis my turn
To make reply. Then having heard me, judge.
OEDIPUS
Thou art glib of tongue, but I am slow to learn
Of thee; I know too well thy venomous hate.
CREON
First I would argue out this very point.
OEDIPUS
O argue not that thou art not a rogue.
CREON
If thou dost count a virtue stubbornness,
Unschooled by reason, thou art much astray.
OEDIPUS
If thou dost hold a kinsman may be wronged,
And no pains follow, thou art much to seek.
CREON
Therein thou judgest rightly, but this wrong
That thou allegest—tell me what it is.
OEDIPUS
Didst thou or didst thou not advise that I
Should call the priest?
CREON
       Yes, and I stand to it.
OEDIPUS
Tell me how long is it since Laius...
CREON
Since Laius...? I follow not thy drift.
OEDIPUS
By violent hands was spirited away.
CREON
In the dim past, a many years agone.
OEDIPUS

Did the same prophet then pursue his craft?
CREON
Yes, skilled as now and in no less repute.
OEDIPUS
Did he at that time ever glance at me?
CREON
Not to my knowledge, not when I was by
OEDIPUS
But was no search and inquisition made?
CREON
Surely full quest was made, but nothing learnt.
OEDIPUS
Why failed the seer to tell his story then?
CREON
I know not, and not knowing hold my tongue.
OEDIPUS
This much thou knowest and canst surely tell.
CREON
What's mean'st thou? All I know I will declare.
OEDIPUS
But for thy prompting never had the seer
Ascribed to me the death of Laius.
CREON
If so he thou knowest best; but I
Would put thee to the question in my turn.
OEDIPUS
Question and prove me murderer if thou canst.
CREON
Then let me ask thee, didst thou wed my sister?
OEDIPUS
A fact so plain I cannot well deny.
CREON
And as thy consort queen she shares the throne?
OEDIPUS
I grant her freely all her heart desires.
CREON

And with you twain I share the triple rule?
OEDIPUS
Yea, and it is that proves thee a false friend.
CREON
Not so, if thou wouldst reason with thyself,
As I with myself. First, I bid thee think,
Would any mortal choose a troubled reign
Of terrors rather than secure repose,
If the same power were given him? As for me,
I have no natural craving for the name
Of king, preferring to do kingly deeds,
And so thinks every sober-minded man.
Now all my needs are satisfied through thee,
And I have naught to fear; but were I king,
My acts would oft run counter to my will.
How could a title then have charms for me
Above the sweets of boundless influence?
I am not so infatuate as to grasp
The shadow when I hold the substance fast.
Now all men cry me Godspeed! wish me well,
And every suitor seeks to gain my ear,
If he would hope to win a grace from thee.
Why should I leave the better, choose the worse?
That were sheer madness, and I am not mad.
No such ambition ever tempted me,
Nor would I have a share in such intrigue.
And if thou doubt me, first to Delphi go,
There ascertain if my report was true
Of the god's answer; next investigate
If with the seer I plotted or conspired,

And if it prove so, sentence me to death,
Not by thy voice alone, but mine and thine.
But O condemn me not, without appeal,
On bare suspicion. 'Tis not right to adjudge
Bad men at random good, or good men bad.
I would as lief a man should cast away
The thing he counts most precious, his own life,
As spurn a true friend. Thou wilt learn in time
The truth, for time alone reveals the just;
A villain is detected in a day.
CHORUS
To one who walketh warily his words
Commend themselves; swift counsels are not sure.
OEDIPUS
When with swift strides the stealthy plotter stalks
I must be quick too with my counterplot.
To wait his onset passively, for him
Is sure success, for me assured defeat.
CREON
What then's thy will? To banish me the land?
OEDIPUS
I would not have thee banished, no, but dead,
That men may mark the wages envy reaps.
CREON
I see thou wilt not yield, nor credit me.
OEDIPUS
[None but a fool would credit such as thou.] 3
CREON
Thou art not wise.
OEDIPUS
       Wise for myself at least.
CREON
Why not for me too?
OEDIPUS

17

Why for such a knave?
CREON
Suppose thou lackest sense.
OEDIPUS
                    Yet kings must rule.
CREON
Not if they rule ill.
OEDIPUS
                    Oh my Thebans, hear him!
CREON
Thy Thebans? am not I a Theban too?
CHORUS
Cease, princes; lo there comes, and none
too soon,
Jocasta from the palace. Who so fit
As peacemaker to reconcile your feud?
[Enter JOCASTA.]
JOCASTA
Misguided princes, why have ye
upraised
This wordy wrangle? Are ye not
ashamed,
While the whole land lies striken, thus to
voice
Your private injuries? Go in, my lord;
Go home, my brother, and forebear to
make
A public scandal of a petty grief.
CREON
My royal sister, Oedipus, thy lord,
Hath bid me choose (O dread
alternative!)
An outlaw's exile or a felon's death.
OEDIPUS
Yes, lady; I have caught him practicing
Against my royal person his vile arts.
CREON
May I ne'er speed but die accursed, if I
In any way am guilty of this charge.
JOCASTA
Believe him, I adjure thee, Oedipus,
First for his solemn oath's sake, then for
mine,
And for thine elders' sake who wait on
thee.

CHORUS
(Str. 1)
Hearken, King, reflect, we pray thee, but
not stubborn but relent.
OEDIPUS
Say to what should I consent?
CHORUS
Respect a man whose probity and troth
Are known to all and now confirmed by
oath.
OEDIPUS
Dost know what grace thou cravest?
CHORUS
                    Yea, I know.
OEDIPUS
Declare it then and make thy meaning
plain.
CHORUS
Brand not a friend whom babbling
tongues assail;
Let not suspicion 'gainst his oath prevail
OEDIPUS
Bethink you that in seeking this ye seek
In very sooth my death or banishment?
CHORUS
No, by the leader of the host divine!
(Str. 2)
Witness, thou Sun, such thought was
never mine,
Unblest, unfriended may I perish,
If ever I such wish did cherish!
But O my heart is desolate
Musing on our striken State,
Doubly fall'n should discord grow
Twixt you twain, to crown our woe.
OEDIPUS
Well, let him go, no matter what it cost
me,
Or certain death or shameful
banishment,
For your sake I relent, not his; and him,
Where'er he be, my heart shall still
abhor.
CREON
Thou art as sullen in thy yielding mood

As in thine anger thou wast truculent.
Such tempers justly plague themselves
the most.
OEDIPUS
Leave me in peace and get thee gone.
CREON
                I go,
By thee misjudged, but justified by these.
[Exeunt CREON]
CHORUS
(Ant. 1)
Lady, lead indoors thy consort;
wherefore longer here delay?
JOCASTA
Tell me first how rose the fray.
CHORUS
Rumors bred unjust suspicious and
injustice rankles sore.
JOCASTA
Were both at fault?
CHORUS
              Both.
JOCASTA
              What was the tale?
CHORUS
Ask me no more. The land is sore
distressed;
'Twere better sleeping ills to leave at
rest.
OEDIPUS
Strange counsel, friend! I know thou
mean'st me well,
And yet would'st mitigate and blunt my
zeal.
CHORUS
(Ant. 2)
King, I say it once again,
Witless were I proved, insane,
If I lightly put away
Thee my country's prop and stay,
Pilot who, in danger sought,
To a quiet haven brought
Our distracted State; and now
Who can guide us right but thou?
JOCASTA

Let me too, I adjure thee, know, O king,
What cause has stirred this unrelenting
wrath.
OEDIPUS
I will, for thou art more to me than these.
Lady, the cause is Creon and his plots.
JOCASTA
But what provoked the quarrel? make
this clear.
OEDIPUS
He points me out as Laius' murderer.
JOCASTA
Of his own knowledge or upon report?
OEDIPUS
He is too cunning to commit himself,
And makes a mouthpiece of a knavish
seer.
JOCASTA
Then thou mayest ease thy conscience
on that score.
Listen and I'll convince thee that no man
Hath scot or lot in the prophetic art.
Here is the proof in brief. An oracle
Once came to Laius (I will not say
'Twas from the Delphic god himself, but
from
His ministers) declaring he was doomed
To perish by the hand of his own son,
A child that should be born to him by me.
Now Laius—so at least report
affirmed—
Was murdered on a day by highwaymen,
No natives, at a spot where three roads
meet.
As for the child, it was but three days
old,
When Laius, its ankles pierced and
pinned
Together, gave it to be cast away
By others on the trackless mountain
side.
So then Apollo brought it not to pass
The child should be his father's
murderer,

Or the dread terror find accomplishment,
And Laius be slain by his own son.
Such was the prophet's horoscope. O king,
Regard it not. Whate'er the god deems fit
To search, himself unaided will reveal.
OEDIPUS
What memories, what wild tumult of the soul
Came o'er me, lady, as I heard thee speak!
JOCASTA
What mean'st thou? What has shocked and startled thee?
OEDIPUS
Methought I heard thee say that Laius
Was murdered at the meeting of three roads.
JOCASTA
So ran the story that is current still.
OEDIPUS
Where did this happen? Dost thou know the place?
JOCASTA
Phocis the land is called; the spot is where
Branch roads from Delphi and from Daulis meet.
OEDIPUS
And how long is it since these things befell?
JOCASTA
'Twas but a brief while were thou wast proclaimed
Our country's ruler that the news was brought.
OEDIPUS
O Zeus, what hast thou willed to do with me!
JOCASTA
What is it, Oedipus, that moves thee so?
OEDIPUS

Ask me not yet; tell me the build and height
Of Laius? Was he still in manhood's prime?
JOCASTA
Tall was he, and his hair was lightly strewn
With silver; and not unlike thee in form.
OEDIPUS
O woe is me! Mehtinks unwittingly
I laid but now a dread curse on myself.
JOCASTA
What say'st thou? When I look upon thee, my king,
I tremble.
OEDIPUS
        'Tis a dread presentiment
That in the end the seer will prove not blind.
One further question to resolve my doubt.
JOCASTA
I quail; but ask, and I will answer all.
OEDIPUS
Had he but few attendants or a train
Of armed retainers with him, like a prince?
JOCASTA
They were but five in all, and one of them
A herald; Laius in a mule-car rode.
OEDIPUS
Alas! 'tis clear as noonday now. But say,
Lady, who carried this report to Thebes?
JOCASTA
A serf, the sole survivor who returned.
OEDIPUS
Haply he is at hand or in the house?
JOCASTA
No, for as soon as he returned and found
Thee reigning in the stead of Laius slain,
He clasped my hand and supplicated me
To send him to the alps and pastures, where

He might be farthest from the sight of
Thebes.
And so I sent him. 'Twas an honest slave
And well deserved some better
recompense.

OEDIPUS
Fetch him at once. I fain would see the
man.

JOCASTA
He shall be brought; but wherefore
summon him?

OEDIPUS
Lady, I fear my tongue has overrun
Discretion; therefore I would question
him.

JOCASTA
Well, he shall come, but may not I too
claim
To share the burden of thy heart, my
king?

OEDIPUS
And thou shalt not be frustrate of thy
wish.
Now my imaginings have gone so far.
Who has a higher claim that thou to hear
My tale of dire adventures? Listen then.
My sire was Polybus of Corinth, and
My mother Merope, a Dorian;
And I was held the foremost citizen,
Till a strange thing befell me, strange
indeed,
Yet scarce deserving all the heat it
stirred.
A roisterer at some banquet, flown with
wine,
Shouted "Thou art not true son of thy
sire."
It irked me, but I stomached for the
nonce
The insult; on the morrow I sought out
My mother and my sire and questioned
them.
They were indignant at the random slur
Cast on my parentage and did their best
To comfort me, but still the venomed
barb
Rankled, for still the scandal spread and
grew.
So privily without their leave I went
To Delphi, and Apollo sent me back
Baulked of the knowledge that I came to
seek.
But other grievous things he prophesied,
Woes, lamentations, mourning, portents
dire;
To wit I should defile my mother's bed
And raise up seed too loathsome to
behold,
And slay the father from whose loins I
sprang.
Then, lady,—thou shalt hear the very
truth—
As I drew near the triple-branching
roads,
A herald met me and a man who sat
In a car drawn by colts—as in thy tale—
The man in front and the old man
himself
Threatened to thrust me rudely from the
path,
Then jostled by the charioteer in wrath
I struck him, and the old man, seeing
this,
Watched till I passed and from his car
brought down
Full on my head the double-pointed
goad.
     Yet was I quits with him and more;
one stroke
Of my good staff sufficed to fling him
clean
Out of the chariot seat and laid him
prone.
And so I slew them every one. But if
Betwixt this stranger there was aught in
common
With Laius, who more miserable than I,
What mortal could you find more god-
abhorred?

Wretch whom no sojourner, no citizen
May harbor or address, whom all are bound
To harry from their homes. And this same curse
Was laid on me, and laid by none but me.
Yea with these hands all gory I pollute
The bed of him I slew. Say, am I vile?
Am I not utterly unclean, a wretch
Doomed to be banished, and in banishment
Forgo the sight of all my dearest ones,
And never tread again my native earth;
Or else to wed my mother and slay my sire,
Polybus, who begat me and upreared?
If one should say, this is the handiwork
Of some inhuman power, who could blame
His judgment? But, ye pure and awful gods,
Forbid, forbid that I should see that day!
May I be blotted out from living men
Ere such a plague spot set on me its brand!

CHORUS
We too, O king, are troubled; but till thou
Hast questioned the survivor, still hope on.

OEDIPUS
My hope is faint, but still enough survives
To bid me bide the coming of this herd.

JOCASTA
Suppose him here, what wouldst thou learn of him?

OEDIPUS
I'll tell thee, lady; if his tale agrees
With thine, I shall have 'scaped calamity.

JOCASTA
And what of special import did I say?

OEDIPUS
In thy report of what the herdsman said
Laius was slain by robbers; now if he
Still speaks of robbers, not a robber, I

Slew him not; "one" with "many" cannot square.
But if he says one lonely wayfarer,
The last link wanting to my guilt is forged.

JOCASTA
Well, rest assured, his tale ran thus at first,
Nor can he now retract what then he said;
Not I alone but all our townsfolk heard it
E'en should he vary somewhat in his story,
He cannot make the death of Laius
In any wise jump with the oracle.
For Loxias said expressly he was doomed
To die by my child's hand, but he, poor babe,
He shed no blood, but perished first himself.
So much for divination. Henceforth I
Will look for signs neither to right nor left.

OEDIPUS
Thou reasonest well. Still I would have thee send
And fetch the bondsman hither. See to it.

JOCASTA
That will I straightway. Come, let us within.
I would do nothing that my lord mislikes.
[Exeunt OEDIPUS and JOCASTA]

CHORUS
(Str. 1)
My lot be still to lead
    The life of innocence and fly
Irreverence in word or deed,
    To follow still those laws ordained on high
Whose birthplace is the bright ethereal sky
    No mortal birth they own,
    Olympus their progenitor alone:
Ne'er shall they slumber in oblivion cold,

The god in them is strong and grows not old.
(Ant. 1)
  Of insolence is bred
The tyrant; insolence full blown,
  With empty riches surfeited,
Scales the precipitous height and grasps the throne.
  Then topples o'er and lies in ruin prone;
  No foothold on that dizzy steep.
But O may Heaven the true patriot keep
Who burns with emulous zeal to serve the State.
God is my help and hope, on him I wait.
(Str. 2)
But the proud sinner, or in word or deed,
  That will not Justice heed,
  Nor reverence the shrine
  Of images divine,
Perdition seize his vain imaginings,
  If, urged by greed profane,
  He grasps at ill-got gain,
And lays an impious hand on holiest things.
  Who when such deeds are done
  Can hope heaven's bolts to shun?
If sin like this to honor can aspire,
Why dance I still and lead the sacred choir?
(Ant. 2)
No more I'll seek earth's central oracle,
  Or Abae's hallowed cell,
  Nor to Olympia bring
  My votive offering.
If before all God's truth be not bade plain.
  O Zeus, reveal thy might,
  King, if thou'rt named aright
Omnipotent, all-seeing, as of old;
  For Laius is forgot;
  His weird, men heed it not;
Apollo is forsook and faith grows cold.
[Enter JOCASTA.]
JOCASTA

My lords, ye look amazed to see your queen
With wreaths and gifts of incense in her hands.
I had a mind to visit the high shrines,
For Oedipus is overwrought, alarmed
With terrors manifold. He will not use
His past experience, like a man of sense,
To judge the present need, but lends an ear
To any croaker if he augurs ill.
Since then my counsels naught avail, I turn
To thee, our present help in time of trouble,
Apollo, Lord Lycean, and to thee
My prayers and supplications here I bring.
Lighten us, lord, and cleanse us from this curse!
For now we all are cowed like mariners
Who see their helmsman dumbstruck in the storm.
[Enter Corinthian MESSENGER.]
MESSENGER
My masters, tell me where the palace is
Of Oedipus; or better, where's the king.
CHORUS
Here is the palace and he bides within;
This is his queen the mother of his children.
MESSENGER
All happiness attend her and the house,
Blessed is her husband and her marriage-bed.
JOCASTA
My greetings to thee, stranger; thy fair words
Deserve a like response. But tell me why
Thou comest—what thy need or what thy news.
MESSENGER
Good for thy consort and the royal house.
JOCASTA

What may it be? Whose messenger art
thou?
MESSENGER
The Isthmian commons have resolved to
make
Thy husband king—so 'twas reported
there.
JOCASTA
What! is not aged Polybus still king?
MESSENGER
No, verily; he's dead and in his grave.
JOCASTA
What! is he dead, the sire of Oedipus?
MESSENGER
If I speak falsely, may I die myself.
JOCASTA
Quick, maiden, bear these tidings to my
lord.
Ye god-sent oracles, where stand ye
now!
This is the man whom Oedipus long
shunned,
In dread to prove his murderer; and now
He dies in nature's course, not by his
hand.
[Enter OEDIPUS.]
OEDIPUS
My wife, my queen, Jocasta, why hast
thou
Summoned me from my palace?
JOCASTA
Hear this man,
And as thou hearest judge what has
become
Of all those awe-inspiring oracles.
OEDIPUS
Who is this man, and what his news for
me?
JOCASTA
He comes from Corinth and his message
this:
Thy father Polybus hath passed away.
OEDIPUS
What? let me have it, stranger, from thy
mouth.

MESSENGER
If I must first make plain beyond a doubt
My message, know that Polybus is dead.
OEDIPUS
By treachery, or by sickness visited?
MESSENGER
One touch will send an old man to his
rest.
OEDIPUS
So of some malady he died, poor man.
MESSENGER
Yes, having measured the full span of
years.
OEDIPUS
Out on it, lady! why should one regard
The Pythian hearth or birds that scream
i' the air?
Did they not point at me as doomed to
slay
My father? but he's dead and in his grave
And here am I who ne'er unsheathed a
sword;
Unless the longing for his absent son
Killed him and so I slew him in a sense.
But, as they stand, the oracles are
dead—
Dust, ashes, nothing, dead as Polybus.
JOCASTA
Say, did not I foretell this long ago?
OEDIPUS
Thou didst: but I was misled by my fear.
JOCASTA
Then let I no more weigh upon thy soul.
OEDIPUS
Must I not fear my mother's marriage
bed.
JOCASTA
Why should a mortal man, the sport of
chance,
With no assured foreknowledge, be
afraid?
Best live a careless life from hand to
mouth.
This wedlock with thy mother fear not
thou.

How oft it chances that in dreams a man
Has wed his mother! He who least regards
Such brainsick phantasies lives most at ease.

OEDIPUS
I should have shared in full thy confidence,
Were not my mother living; since she lives
Though half convinced I still must live in dread.

JOCASTA
And yet thy sire's death lights out darkness much.

OEDIPUS
Much, but my fear is touching her who lives.

MESSENGER
Who may this woman be whom thus you fear?

OEDIPUS
Merope, stranger, wife of Polybus.

MESSENGER
And what of her can cause you any fear?

OEDIPUS
A heaven-sent oracle of dread import.

MESSENGER
A mystery, or may a stranger hear it?

OEDIPUS
Aye, 'tis no secret. Loxias once foretold
That I should mate with mine own mother, and shed
With my own hands the blood of my own sire.
Hence Corinth was for many a year to me
A home distant; and I trove abroad,
But missed the sweetest sight, my parents' face.

MESSENGER
Was this the fear that exiled thee from home?

OEDIPUS
Yea, and the dread of slaying my own sire.

MESSENGER
Why, since I came to give thee pleasure, King,
Have I not rid thee of this second fear?

OEDIPUS
Well, thou shalt have due guerdon for thy pains.

MESSENGER
Well, I confess what chiefly made me come
Was hope to profit by thy coming home.

OEDIPUS
Nay, I will ne'er go near my parents more.

MESSENGER
My son, 'tis plain, thou know'st not what thou doest.

OEDIPUS
How so, old man? For heaven's sake tell me all.

MESSENGER
If this is why thou dreadest to return.

OEDIPUS
Yea, lest the god's word be fulfilled in me.

MESSENGER
Lest through thy parents thou shouldst be accursed?

OEDIPUS
This and none other is my constant dread.

MESSENGER
Dost thou not know thy fears are baseless all?

OEDIPUS
How baseless, if I am their very son?

MESSENGER
Since Polybus was naught to thee in blood.

OEDIPUS
What say'st thou? was not Polybus my sire?

MESSENGER

As much thy sire as I am, and no more.
OEDIPUS
My sire no more to me than one who is naught?
MESSENGER
Since I begat thee not, no more did he.
OEDIPUS
What reason had he then to call me son?
MESSENGER
Know that he took thee from my hands, a gift.
OEDIPUS
Yet, if no child of his, he loved me well.
MESSENGER
A childless man till then, he warmed to thee.
OEDIPUS
A foundling or a purchased slave, this child?
MESSENGER
I found thee in Cithaeron's wooded glens.
OEDIPUS
What led thee to explore those upland glades?
MESSENGER
My business was to tend the mountain flocks.
OEDIPUS
A vagrant shepherd journeying for hire?
MESSENGER
True, but thy savior in that hour, my son.
OEDIPUS
My savior? from what harm? what ailed me then?
MESSENGER
Those ankle joints are evidence enow.
OEDIPUS
Ah, why remind me of that ancient sore?
MESSENGER
I loosed the pin that riveted thy feet.
OEDIPUS
Yes, from my cradle that dread brand I bore.
MESSENGER

Whence thou deriv'st the name that still is thine.
OEDIPUS
Who did it? I adjure thee, tell me who
Say, was it father, mother?
MESSENGER
                    I know not.
The man from whom I had thee may know more.
OEDIPUS
What, did another find me, not thyself?
MESSENGER
Not I; another shepherd gave thee me.
OEDIPUS
Who was he? Would'st thou know again the man?
MESSENGER
He passed indeed for one of Laius' house
OEDIPUS
The king who ruled the country long ago?
MESSENGER
The same: he was a herdsman of the king.
OEDIPUS
And is he living still for me to see him?
MESSENGER
His fellow-countrymen should best know that.
OEDIPUS
Doth any bystander among you know
The herd he speaks of, or by seeing him
Afield or in the city? answer straight!
The hour hath come to clear this business up.
CHORUS
Methinks he means none other than the hind
Whom thou anon wert fain to see; but that
Our queen Jocasta best of all could tell.
OEDIPUS
Madam, dost know the man we sent to fetch?

Is the same of whom the stranger speaks?
JOCASTA
Who is the man? What matter? Let it be.
'Twere waste of thought to weigh such idle words.
OEDIPUS
No, with such guiding clues I cannot fail
To bring to light the secret of my birth.
JOCASTA
Oh, as thou carest for thy life, give o'er
This quest. Enough the anguish I endure.
OEDIPUS
Be of good cheer; though I be proved the son
Of a bondwoman, aye, through three descents
Triply a slave, thy honor is unsmirched.
JOCASTA
Yet humor me, I pray thee; do not this.
OEDIPUS
I cannot; I must probe this matter home.
JOCASTA
'Tis for thy sake I advise thee for the best.
OEDIPUS
I grow impatient of this best advice.
JOCASTA
Ah mayst thou ne'er discover who thou art!
OEDIPUS
Go, fetch me here the herd, and leave yon woman
To glory in her pride of ancestry.
JOCASTA
O woe is thee, poor wretch! With that last word
I leave thee, henceforth silent evermore.
[Exit JOCASTA]
CHORUS
Why, Oedipus, why stung with passionate grief
Hath the queen thus departed? Much I fear

From this dead calm will burst a storm of woes.
OEDIPUS
Let the storm burst, my fixed resolve still holds,
To learn my lineage, be it ne'er so low.
It may be she with all a woman's pride
Thinks scorn of my base parentage. But I
Who rank myself as Fortune's favorite child,
The giver of good gifts, shall not be shamed.
She is my mother and the changing moons
My brethren, and with them I wax and wane.
Thus sprung why should I fear to trace my birth?
Nothing can make me other than I am.
CHORUS
(Str.)
If my soul prophetic err not, if my wisdom aught avail,
        Thee, Cithaeron, I shall hail,
As the nurse and foster-mother of our
Oedipus shall greet
Ere tomorrow's full moon rises, and exalt thee as is meet.
Dance and song shall hymn thy praises, lover of our royal race.
        Phoebus, may my words find grace!
(Ant.)
Child, who bare thee, nymph or goddess? sure thy sure was more than man,
        Haply the hill-roamer Pan.
Of did Loxias beget thee, for he haunts the upland wold;
Or Cyllene's lord, or Bacchus, dweller on the hilltops cold?
Did some Heliconian Oread give him thee, a new-born joy?
        Nymphs with whom he love to toy?
OEDIPUS

27

Elders, if I, who never yet before
Have met the man, may make a guess, methinks
I see the herdsman who we long have sought;
His time-worn aspect matches with the years
Of yonder aged messenger; besides
I seem to recognize the men who bring him
As servants of my own. But you, perchance,
Having in past days known or seen the herd,
May better by sure knowledge my surmise.
CHORUS
I recognize him; one of Laius' house;
A simple hind, but true as any man.
[Enter HERDSMAN.]
OEDIPUS
Corinthian, stranger, I address thee first,
Is this the man thou meanest!
MESSENGER
                    This is he.
OEDIPUS
And now old man, look up and answer all
I ask thee. Wast thou once of Laius' house?
HERDSMAN
I was, a thrall, not purchased but home-bred.
OEDIPUS
What was thy business? how wast thou employed?
HERDSMAN
The best part of my life I tended sheep.
OEDIPUS
What were the pastures thou didst most frequent?
HERDSMAN
Cithaeron and the neighboring alps.
OEDIPUS
                    Then there

Thou must have known yon man, at least by fame?
HERDSMAN
Yon man? in what way? what man dost thou mean?
OEDIPUS
The man here, having met him in past times...
HERDSMAN
Off-hand I cannot call him well to mind.
MESSENGER
No wonder, master. But I will revive
His blunted memories. Sure he can recall
What time together both we drove our flocks,
He two, I one, on the Cithaeron range,
For three long summers; I his mate from spring
Till rose Arcturus; then in winter time
I led mine home, he his to Laius' folds.
Did these things happen as I say, or no?
HERDSMAN
'Tis long ago, but all thou say'st is true.
MESSENGER
Well, thou mast then remember giving me
A child to rear as my own foster-son?
HERDSMAN
Why dost thou ask this question? What of that?
MESSENGER
Friend, he that stands before thee was that child.
HERDSMAN
A plague upon thee! Hold thy wanton tongue!
OEDIPUS
Softly, old man, rebuke him not; thy words
Are more deserving chastisement than his.
HERDSMAN
O best of masters, what is my offense?
OEDIPUS

Not answering what he asks about the child.

HERDSMAN
He speaks at random, babbles like a fool.

OEDIPUS
If thou lack'st grace to speak, I'll loose thy tongue.

HERDSMAN
For mercy's sake abuse not an old man.

OEDIPUS
Arrest the villain, seize and pinion him!

HERDSMAN
Alack, alack!
What have I done? what wouldst thou further learn?

OEDIPUS
Didst give this man the child of whom he asks?

HERDSMAN
I did; and would that I had died that day!

OEDIPUS
And die thou shalt unless thou tell the truth.

HERDSMAN
But, if I tell it, I am doubly lost.

OEDIPUS
The knave methinks will still prevaricate.

HERDSMAN
Nay, I confessed I gave it long ago.

OEDIPUS
Whence came it? was it thine, or given to thee?

HERDSMAN
I had it from another, 'twas not mine.

OEDIPUS
From whom of these our townsmen, and what house?

HERDSMAN
Forbear for God's sake, master, ask no more.

OEDIPUS
If I must question thee again, thou'rt lost.

HERDSMAN
Well then—it was a child of Laius' house.

OEDIPUS
Slave-born or one of Laius' own race?

HERDSMAN
Ah me!
I stand upon the perilous edge of speech.

OEDIPUS
And I of hearing, but I still must hear.

HERDSMAN
Know then the child was by repute his own,
But she within, thy consort best could tell.

OEDIPUS
What! she, she gave it thee?

HERDSMAN
            'Tis so, my king.

OEDIPUS
With what intent?

HERDSMAN
          To make away with it.

OEDIPUS
What, she its mother.

HERDSMAN
          Fearing a dread weird.

OEDIPUS
What weird?

HERDSMAN
      'Twas told that he should slay his sire.

OEDIPUS
What didst thou give it then to this old man?

HERDSMAN
Through pity, master, for the babe. I thought
He'd take it to the country whence he came;
But he preserved it for the worst of woes.
For if thou art in sooth what this man saith,
God pity thee! thou wast to misery born.

OEDIPUS
Ah me! ah me! all brought to pass, all true!

O light, may I behold thee nevermore!
I stand a wretch, in birth, in wedlock cursed,
A parricide, incestuously, triply cursed!
[Exit OEDIPUS]
CHORUS
(Str. 1)

> Races of mortal man
> Whose life is but a span,

I count ye but the shadow of a shade!

> For he who most doth know
> Of bliss, hath but the show;

A moment, and the visions pale and fade.
Thy fall, O Oedipus, thy piteous fall
Warns me none born of women blest to call.
(Ant. 1)

> For he of marksmen best,
> O Zeus, outshot the rest,

And won the prize supreme of wealth and power.

> By him the vulture maid
> Was quelled, her witchery laid;

He rose our savior and the land's strong tower.
We hailed thee king and from that day adored
Of mighty Thebes the universal lord.
(Str. 2)

> O heavy hand of fate!
> Who now more desolate,

Whose tale more sad than thine, whose lot more dire?

> O Oedipus, discrowned head,
> Thy cradle was thy marriage bed;

One harborage sufficed for son and sire.
How could the soil thy father eared so long
Endure to bear in silence such a wrong?
(Ant. 2)

> All-seeing Time hath caught
> Guilt, and to justice brought

The son and sire commingled in one bed.

> O child of Laius' ill-starred race
> Would I had ne'er beheld thy face;

I raise for thee a dirge as o'er the dead.
Yet, sooth to say, through thee I drew new breath,
And now through thee I feel a second death.
[Enter SECOND MESSENGER.]
SECOND MESSENGER
Most grave and reverend senators of Thebes,
What Deeds ye soon must hear, what sights behold
How will ye mourn, if, true-born patriots,
Ye reverence still the race of Labdacus!
Not Ister nor all Phasis' flood, I ween,
Could wash away the blood-stains from this house,
The ills it shrouds or soon will bring to light,
Ills wrought of malice, not unwittingly.
The worst to bear are self-inflicted wounds.
CHORUS
Grievous enough for all our tears and groans
Our past calamities; what canst thou add?
SECOND MESSENGER
My tale is quickly told and quickly heard.
Our sovereign lady queen Jocasta's dead.
CHORUS
Alas, poor queen! how came she by her death?
SECOND MESSENGER
By her own hand. And all the horror of it,
Not having seen, yet cannot comprehend.
Nathless, as far as my poor memory serves,
I will relate the unhappy lady's woe.
When in her frenzy she had passed inside
The vestibule, she hurried straight to win

30

The bridal-chamber, clutching at her
hair
With both her hands, and, once within
the room,
She shut the doors behind her with a
crash.
"Laius," she cried, and called her
husband dead
Long, long ago; her thought was of that
child
By him begot, the son by whom the sire
Was murdered and the mother left to
breed
With her own seed, a monstrous
progeny.
Then she bewailed the marriage bed
whereon
Poor wretch, she had conceived a double
brood,
Husband by husband, children by her
child.
What happened after that I cannot tell,
Nor how the end befell, for with a shriek
Burst on us Oedipus; all eyes were fixed
On Oedipus, as up and down he strode,
Nor could we mark her agony to the end.
For stalking to and fro "A sword!" he
cried,
"Where is the wife, no wife, the teeming
womb
That bore a double harvest, me and
mine?"
And in his frenzy some supernal power
(No mortal, surely, none of us who
watched him)
Guided his footsteps; with a terrible
shriek,
As though one beckoned him, he crashed
against
The folding doors, and from their staples
forced
The wrenched bolts and hurled himself
within.
Then we beheld the woman hanging
there,

A running noose entwined about her
neck.
But when he saw her, with a maddened
roar
He loosed the cord; and when her
wretched corpse
Lay stretched on earth, what followed—
O 'twas dread!
He tore the golden brooches that upheld
Her queenly robes, upraised them high
and smote
Full on his eye-balls, uttering words like
these:
"No more shall ye behold such sights of
woe,
Deeds I have suffered and myself have
wrought;
Henceforward quenched in darkness
shall ye see
Those ye should ne'er have seen; now
blind to those
Whom, when I saw, I vainly yearned to
know."
    Such was the burden of his moan,
whereto,
Not once but oft, he struck with his hand
uplift
His eyes, and at each stroke the
ensanguined orbs
Bedewed his beard, not oozing drop by
drop,
But one black gory downpour, thick as
hail.
Such evils, issuing from the double
source,
Have whelmed them both, confounding
man and wife.
Till now the storied fortune of this house
Was fortunate indeed; but from this day
Woe, lamentation, ruin, death, disgrace,
All ills that can be named, all, all are
theirs.
CHORUS
But hath he still no respite from his
pain?

31

SECOND MESSENGER
He cries, "Unbar the doors and let all
Thebes
Behold the slayer of his sire, his
mother's—"
That shameful word my lips may not
repeat.
He vows to fly self-banished from the
land,
Nor stay to bring upon his house the
curse
Himself had uttered; but he has no
strength
Nor one to guide him, and his torture's
more
Than man can suffer, as yourselves will
see.
For lo, the palace portals are unbarred,
And soon ye shall behold a sight so sad
That he who must abhorred would pity
it.
[Enter OEDIPUS blinded.]
CHORUS
    Woeful sight! more woeful none
    These sad eyes have looked upon.
    Whence this madness? None can
tell
    Who did cast on thee his spell,
    prowling all thy life around,
    Leaping with a demon bound.
    Hapless wretch! how can I brook
    On thy misery to look?
    Though to gaze on thee I yearn,
    Much to question, much to learn,
    Horror-struck away I turn.
OEDIPUS
Ah me! ah woe is me!
Ah whither am I borne!
How like a ghost forlorn
My voice flits from me on the air!
On, on the demon goads. The end, ah
where?
CHORUS
An end too dread to tell, too dark to see.
OEDIPUS

(Str. 1)
Dark, dark! The horror of darkness, like
a shroud,
Wraps me and bears me on through mist
and cloud.
Ah me, ah me! What spasms athwart me
shoot,
What pangs of agonizing memory?
CHORUS
No marvel if in such a plight thou feel'st
The double weight of past and present
woes.
OEDIPUS
(Ant. 1)
Ah friend, still loyal, constant still and
kind,
    Thou carest for the blind.
I know thee near, and though bereft of
eyes,
    Thy voice I recognize.
CHORUS
O doer of dread deeds, how couldst thou
mar
Thy vision thus? What demon goaded
thee?
OEDIPUS
(Str. 2)
Apollo, friend, Apollo, he it was
    That brought these ills to pass;
But the right hand that dealt the blow
    Was mine, none other. How,
How, could I longer see when sight
    Brought no delight?
CHORUS
Alas! 'tis as thou sayest.
OEDIPUS
Say, friends, can any look or voice
Or touch of love henceforth my heart
rejoice?
    Haste, friends, no fond delay,
    Take the twice cursed away
    Far from all ken,
The man abhorred of gods, accursed of
men.
CHORUS

O thy despair well suits thy desperate case.
Would I had never looked upon thy face!

OEDIPUS
(Ant. 2)
My curse on him whoe'er unrived
The waif's fell fetters and my life revived!
He meant me well, yet had he left me there,
He had saved my friends and me a world of care.

CHORUS
I too had wished it so.

OEDIPUS
Then had I never come to shed
My father's blood nor climbed my mother's bed;
The monstrous offspring of a womb defiled,
Co-mate of him who gendered me, and child.
Was ever man before afflicted thus,
Like Oedipus.

CHORUS
I cannot say that thou hast counseled well,
For thou wert better dead than living blind.

OEDIPUS
What's done was well done. Thou canst never shake
My firm belief. A truce to argument.
For, had I sight, I know not with what eyes
I could have met my father in the shades,
Or my poor mother, since against the twain
I sinned, a sin no gallows could atone.
Aye, but, ye say, the sight of children joys
A parent's eyes. What, born as mine were born?
No, such a sight could never bring me joy;
Nor this fair city with its battlements,
Its temples and the statues of its gods,
Sights from which I, now wretchedst of all,
Once ranked the foremost Theban in all Thebes,
By my own sentence am cut off, condemned
By my own proclamation 'gainst the wretch,
The miscreant by heaven itself declared
Unclean—and of the race of Laius.
Thus branded as a felon by myself,
How had I dared to look you in the face?
Nay, had I known a way to choke the springs
Of hearing, I had never shrunk to make
A dungeon of this miserable frame,
Cut off from sight and hearing; for 'tis bliss
to bide in regions sorrow cannot reach.
Why didst thou harbor me, Cithaeron, why
Didst thou not take and slay me? Then I never
Had shown to men the secret of my birth.
O Polybus, O Corinth, O my home,
Home of my ancestors (so wast thou called)
How fair a nursling then I seemed, how foul
The canker that lay festering in the bud!
Now is the blight revealed of root and fruit.
Ye triple high-roads, and thou hidden glen,
Coppice, and pass where meet the three-branched ways,
Ye drank my blood, the life-blood these hands spilt,
My father's; do ye call to mind perchance
Those deeds of mine ye witnessed and the work
I wrought thereafter when I came to Thebes?

33

O fatal wedlock, thou didst give me birth,
And, having borne me, sowed again my seed,
Mingling the blood of fathers, brothers, children,
Brides, wives and mothers, an incestuous brood,
All horrors that are wrought beneath the sun,
Horrors so foul to name them were unmeet.
O, I adjure you, hide me anywhere
Far from this land, or slay me straight, or cast me
Down to the depths of ocean out of sight.
Come hither, deign to touch an abject wretch;
Draw near and fear not; I myself must bear
The load of guilt that none but I can share.

[Enter CREON.]

CREON
Lo, here is Creon, the one man to grant
Thy prayer by action or advice, for he
Is left the State's sole guardian in thy stead.

OEDIPUS
Ah me! what words to accost him can I find?
What cause has he to trust me? In the past
I have bee proved his rancorous enemy.

CREON
Not in derision, Oedipus, I come
Nor to upbraid thee with thy past misdeeds.

(To BYSTANDERS)
But shame upon you! if ye feel no sense
Of human decencies, at least revere
The Sun whose light beholds and nurtures all.
Leave not thus nakedly for all to gaze at
A horror neither earth nor rain from heaven

Nor light will suffer. Lead him straight within,
For it is seemly that a kinsman's woes
Be heard by kin and seen by kin alone.

OEDIPUS
O listen, since thy presence comes to me
A shock of glad surprise—so noble thou,
And I so vile—O grant me one small boon.
I ask it not on my behalf, but thine.

CREON
And what the favor thou wouldst crave of me?

OEDIPUS
Forth from thy borders thrust me with all speed;
Set me within some vasty desert where
No mortal voice shall greet me any more

CREON
This had I done already, but I deemed
It first behooved me to consult the god.

OEDIPUS
His will was set forth fully—to destroy
The parricide, the scoundrel; and I am he.

CREON
Yea, so he spake, but in our present plight
'Twere better to consult the god anew.

OEDIPUS
Dare ye inquire concerning such a wretch?

CREON
Yea, for thyself wouldst credit now his word.

OEDIPUS
Aye, and on thee in all humility
I lay this charge: let her who lies within
Receive such burial as thou shalt ordain;
Such rites 'tis thine, as brother, to perform.
But for myself, O never let my Thebes,
The city of my sires, be doomed to bear
The burden of my presence while I live.
No, let me be a dweller on the hills,

On yonder mount Cithaeron, famed as mine,
My tomb predestined for me by my sire
And mother, while they lived, that I may die
Slain as they sought to slay me, when alive.
This much I know full surely, nor disease
Shall end my days, nor any common chance;
For I had ne'er been snatched from death, unless
I was predestined to some awful doom.
　So be it. I reck not how Fate deals with me
But my unhappy children—for my sons
Be not concerned, O Creon, they are men,
And for themselves, where'er they be, can fend.
But for my daughters twain, poor innocent maids,
Who ever sat beside me at the board
Sharing my viands, drinking of my cup,
For them, I pray thee, care, and, if thou willst,
O might I feel their touch and make my moan.
Hear me, O prince, my noble-hearted prince!
Could I but blindly touch them with my hands
I'd think they still were mine, as when I saw.
[ANTIGONE and ISMENE are led in.]
What say I? can it be my pretty ones
Whose sobs I hear? Has Creon pitied me
And sent me my two darlings? Can this be?

CREON
'Tis true; 'twas I procured thee this delight,
Knowing the joy they were to thee of old.

OEDIPUS
God speed thee! and as meed for bringing them

May Providence deal with thee kindlier
Than it has dealt with me! O children mine,
Where are ye? Let me clasp you with these hands,
A brother's hands, a father's; hands that made
Lack-luster sockets of his once bright eyes;
Hands of a man who blindly, recklessly,
Became your sire by her from whom he sprang.
Though I cannot behold you, I must weep
In thinking of the evil days to come,
The slights and wrongs that men will put upon you.
Where'er ye go to feast or festival,
No merrymaking will it prove for you,
But oft abashed in tears ye will return.
And when ye come to marriageable years,
Where's the bold wooers who will jeopardize
To take unto himself such disrepute
As to my children's children still must cling,
For what of infamy is lacking here?
"Their father slew his father, sowed the seed
Where he himself was gendered, and begat
These maidens at the source wherefrom he sprang."
Such are the gibes that men will cast at you.
Who then will wed you? None, I ween, but ye
Must pine, poor maids, in single barrenness.
O Prince, Menoeceus' son, to thee, I turn,
With the it rests to father them, for we
Their natural parents, both of us, are lost.

O leave them not to wander poor, unwed,
Thy kin, nor let them share my low estate.
O pity them so young, and but for thee
All destitute. Thy hand upon it, Prince.
To you, my children I had much to say,
Were ye but ripe to hear. Let this suffice:
Pray ye may find some home and live content,
And may your lot prove happier than your sire's.

CREON
Thou hast had enough of weeping; pass within.

OEDIPUS
                          I must obey,
Though 'tis grievous.

CREON
                 Weep not, everything must have its day.

OEDIPUS
Well I go, but on conditions.

CREON
                          What thy terms for going, say.

OEDIPUS
Send me from the land an exile.

CREON
                          Ask this of the gods, not me.

OEDIPUS
But I am the gods' abhorrence.

CREON
                    Then they soon will grant thy plea.

OEDIPUS
Lead me hence, then, I am willing.

CREON
                          Come, but let thy children go.

OEDIPUS
Rob me not of these my children!

CREON
                    Crave not mastery in all,
For the mastery that raised thee was thy bane and wrought thy fall.

CHORUS
Look ye, countrymen and Thebans, this is Oedipus the great,
He who knew the Sphinx's riddle and was mightiest in our state.
Who of all our townsmen gazed not on his fame with envious eyes?
Now, in what a sea of troubles sunk and overwhelmed he lies!
Therefore wait to see life's ending ere thou count one mortal blest;
Wait till free from pain and sorrow he has gained his final rest.

Notes

1. [Dr. Kennedy and others render "Since to men of experience I see that also comparisons of their counsels are in most lively use."]

2. [Literally "not to call them thine," but the Greek may be rendered "In order not to reveal thine."]

3. [The Greek text that occurs in this place has been lost.]

Oedipus at Colonus

Argument

Oedipus, the blind and banished King of Thebes, has come in his wanderings to Colonus, a deme of Athens, led by his daughter Antigone. He sits to rest on a rock just within a sacred grove of the Furies and is bidden depart by a passing native. But Oedipus, instructed by an oracle that he had reached his final resting-place, refuses to stir, and the stranger consents to go and consult the Elders of Colonus (the Chorus of the Play). Conducted to the spot they pity at first the blind beggar and his daughter, but on learning his name they are horror-striken and order him to quit the land. He appeals to the world-famed hospitality of Athens and hints at the blessings that his coming will confer on the State. They agree to await the decision of King Theseus. From Theseus Oedipus craves protection in life and burial in Attic soil; the benefits that will accrue shall be told later. Theseus departs having promised to aid and befriend him. No sooner has he gone than Creon enters with an armed guard who seize Antigone and carry her off (Ismene, the other sister, they have already captured) and he is about to lay hands on Oedipus, when Theseus, who has heard the tumult, hurries up and, upbraiding Creon for his lawless act, threatens to detain him till he has shown where the captives are and restored them. In the next scene Theseus returns bringing with him the rescued maidens. He informs Oedipus that a stranger who has taken sanctuary at the altar of Poseidon wishes to see him. It is Polyneices who has come to crave his father's forgiveness and blessing, knowing by an oracle that victory will fall to the side that Oedipus espouses. But Oedipus spurns the hypocrite, and invokes a dire curse on both his unnatural sons. A sudden clap of thunder is heard, and as peal follows peal, Oedipus is aware that his hour is come and bids Antigone summon Theseus. Self-guided he leads the way to the spot where death should overtake him, attended by Theseus and his daughters. Halfway he bids his daughters farewell, and what followed none but Theseus knew. He was not (so the Messenger reports) for the gods took him.

Dramatis Personae

OEDIPUS, banished King of Thebes.
ANTIGONE, his daughter.
ISMENE, his daughter.
THESEUS, King of Athens.
CREON, brother of Jocasta, now reigning at Thebes.
POLYNEICES, elder son of Oedipus.
STRANGER, a native of Colonus.
MESSENGER, an attendant of Theseus.
CHORUS, citizens of Colonus.

Scene: In front of the grove of the Eumenides.

Enter the blind OEDIPUS led by his daughter, ANTIGONE.

OEDIPUS
Child of an old blind sire, Antigone,
What region, say, whose city have we reached?
Who will provide today with scanted dole
This wanderer? 'Tis little that he craves,
And less obtains—that less enough for me;
For I am taught by suffering to endure,
And the long years that have grown old with me,
And last not least, by true nobility.
My daughter, if thou seest a resting place
On common ground or by some sacred grove,
Stay me and set me down. Let us discover
Where we have come, for strangers must inquire
Of denizens, and do as they are bid.
ANTIGONE

Long-suffering father, Oedipus, the towers
That fence the city still are faint and far;
But where we stand is surely holy ground;
A wilderness of laurel, olive, vine;
Within a choir or songster nightingales
Are warbling. On this native seat of rock
Rest; for an old man thou hast traveled far.
OEDIPUS
Guide these dark steps and seat me there secure.
ANTIGONE
If time can teach, I need not to be told.
OEDIPUS
Say, prithee, if thou knowest, where we are.
ANTIGONE
Athens I recognize, but not the spot.
OEDIPUS
That much we heard from every wayfarer.
ANTIGONE
Shall I go on and ask about the place?
OEDIPUS
Yes, daughter, if it be inhabited.
ANTIGONE
Sure there are habitations; but no need

38

To leave thee; yonder is a man hard by.
OEDIPUS
What, moving hitherward and on his way?
ANTIGONE
Say rather, here already. Ask him straight
The needful questions, for the man is here.
[Enter STRANGER]
OEDIPUS
O stranger, as I learn from her whose eyes
Must serve both her and me, that thou art here
Sent by some happy chance to serve our doubts—
STRANGER
First quit that seat, then question me at large:
The spot thou treadest on is holy ground.
OEDIPUS
What is the site, to what god dedicate?
STRANGER
Inviolable, untrod; goddesses,
Dread brood of Earth and Darkness, here abide.
OEDIPUS
Tell me the awful name I should invoke?
STRANGER
The Gracious Ones, All-seeing, so our folk
Call them, but elsewhere other names are rife.
OEDIPUS
Then may they show their suppliant grace, for I
From this your sanctuary will ne'er depart.
STRANGER
What word is this?
OEDIPUS
      The watchword of my fate.
STRANGER
Nay, 'tis not mine to bid thee hence without

Due warrant and instruction from the State.
OEDIPUS
Now in God's name, O stranger, scorn me not
As a wayfarer; tell me what I crave.
STRANGER
Ask; your request shall not be scorned by me.
OEDIPUS
How call you then the place wherein we bide?
STRANGER
Whate'er I know thou too shalt know; the place
Is all to great Poseidon consecrate.
Hard by, the Titan, he who bears the torch,
Prometheus, has his worship; but the spot
Thou treadest, the Brass-footed Threshold named,
Is Athens' bastion, and the neighboring lands
Claim as their chief and patron yonder knight
Colonus, and in common bear his name.
Such, stranger, is the spot, to fame unknown,
But dear to us its native worshipers.
OEDIPUS
Thou sayest there are dwellers in these parts?
STRANGER
Surely; they bear the name of yonder god.
OEDIPUS
Ruled by a king or by the general voice?
STRANGER
The lord of Athens is our over-lord.
OEDIPUS
Who is this monarch, great in word and might?
STRANGER
Theseus, the son of Aegeus our late king.

OEDIPUS
Might one be sent from you to summon him?
STRANGER
Wherefore? To tell him aught or urge his coming?
OEDIPUS
Say a slight service may avail him much.
STRANGER
How can he profit from a sightless man?
OEDIPUS
The blind man's words will be instinct with sight.
STRANGER
Heed then; I fain would see thee out of harm;
For by the looks, marred though they be by fate,
I judge thee noble; tarry where thou art,
While I go seek the burghers—those at hand,
Not in the city. They will soon decide
Whether thou art to rest or go thy way.
[Exit STRANGER]
OEDIPUS
Tell me, my daughter, has the stranger gone?
ANTIGONE
Yes, he has gone; now we are all alone,
And thou may'st speak, dear father, without fear.
OEDIPUS
Stern-visaged queens, since coming to this land
First in your sanctuary I bent the knee,
Frown not on me or Phoebus, who, when erst
He told me all my miseries to come,
Spake of this respite after many years,
Some haven in a far-off land, a rest
Vouchsafed at last by dread divinities.
"There," said he, "shalt thou round thy weary life,
A blessing to the land wherein thou dwell'st,

But to the land that cast thee forth, a curse."
And of my weird he promised signs should come,
Earthquake, or thunderclap, or lightning flash.
And now I recognize as yours the sign
That led my wanderings to this your grove;
Else had I never lighted on you first,
A wineless man on your seat of native rock.
O goddesses, fulfill Apollo's word,
Grant me some consummation of my life
If haply I appear not all too vile,
A thrall to sorrow worse than any slave.
Hear, gentle daughters of primeval Night,
Hear, namesake of great Pallas; Athens, first
Of cities, pity this dishonored shade,
The ghost of him who once was Oedipus.
ANTIGONE
Hush! for I see some grey-beards on their way,
Their errand to spy out our resting-place.
OEDIPUS
I will be mute, and thou shalt guide my steps
Into the covert from the public road,
Till I have learned their drift. A prudent man
Will ever shape his course by what he learns.
[Enter CHORUS]
CHORUS
(Str. 1)
Ha! Where is he? Look around!
Every nook and corner scan!
He the all-presumptuous man,
Whither vanished? search the ground!
A wayfarer, I ween,
A wayfarer, no countryman of ours,
That old man must have been;

40

Never had native dared to tempt the Powers,
Or enter their demesne,
The Maids in awe of whom each mortal cowers,
Whose name no voice betrays nor cry,
And as we pass them with averted eye,
We move hushed lips in reverent piety.
But now some godless man,
'Tis rumored, here abides;
The precincts through I scan,
Yet wot not where he hides,
The wretch profane!
I search and search in vain.

OEDIPUS
I am that man; I know you near
Ears to the blind, they say, are eyes.

CHORUS
O dread to see and dread to hear!

OEDIPUS
Oh sirs, I am no outlaw under ban.

CHORUS
Who can he be—Zeus save us!—this old man?

OEDIPUS
No favorite of fate,
That ye should envy his estate,
O, Sirs, would any happy mortal, say,
Grope by the light of other eyes his way,
Or face the storm upon so frail a stay?

CHORUS
(Ant. 1)
Wast thou then sightless from thy birth?
Evil, methinks, and long
Thy pilgrimage on earth.
Yet add not curse to curse and wrong to wrong.
I warn thee, trespass not
Within this hallowed spot,
Lest thou shouldst find the silent grassy glade
Where offerings are laid,

Bowls of spring water mingled with sweet mead.
Thou must not stay,
Come, come away,
Tired wanderer, dost thou heed?
(We are far off, but sure our voice can reach.)
If aught thou wouldst beseech,
Speak where 'tis right; till then refrain from speech.

OEDIPUS
Daughter, what counsel should we now pursue?

ANTIGONE
We must obey and do as here they do.

OEDIPUS
Thy hand then!

ANTIGONE
Here, O father, is my hand,

OEDIPUS
O Sirs, if I come forth at your command,
Let me not suffer for my confidence.

CHORUS
(Str. 2)
Against thy will no man shall drive thee hence.

OEDIPUS
Shall I go further?

CHORUS
Aye.

OEDIPUS
What further still?

CHORUS
Lead maiden, thou canst guide him where we will.

ANTIGONE
Follow with blind steps, father, as I lead.

CHORUS
In a strange land strange thou art;
To her will incline thy heart;
Honor whatso'er the State
Honors, all she frowns on hate.

OEDIPUS
Guide me child, where we may range
Safe within the paths of right;

Counsel freely may exchange
Nor with fate and fortune fight.
CHORUS
(Ant. 2)
Halt! Go no further than that rocky floor.
OEDIPUS
Stay where I now am?
CHORUS
            Yes, advance no more.
OEDIPUS
May I sit down?
CHORUS
            Move sideways towards the
ledge,
And sit thee crouching on the scarped
edge.
ANTIGONE
This is my office, father, O incline—
OEDIPUS
Ah me! ah me!
ANTIGONE
Thy steps to my steps, lean thine aged
frame on mine.
OEDIPUS
Woe on my fate unblest!
CHORUS
Wanderer, now thou art at rest,
Tell me of thy birth and home,
From what far country art thou come,
Led on thy weary way, declare!
OEDIPUS
Strangers, I have no country. O
forbear—
CHORUS
What is it, old man, that thou wouldst
conceal?
OEDIPUS
Forbear, nor urge me further to reveal—
CHORUS
Why this reluctance?
OEDIPUS
            Dread my lineage.
CHORUS
                        Say!
OEDIPUS

What must I answer, child, ah welladay!
CHORUS
Say of what stock thou comest, what
man's son—
OEDIPUS
Ah me, my daughter, now we are
undone!
ANTIGONE
Speak, for thou standest on the slippery
verge.
OEDIPUS
I will; no plea for silence can I urge.
CHORUS
Will neither speak? Come, Sir, why dally
thus!
OEDIPUS
Know'st one of Laius'—
CHORUS
                        Ha? Who!
OEDIPUS
Seed of Labdacus—
CHORUS
                        Oh Zeus!
OEDIPUS
The hapless Oedipus.
CHORUS
                        Art he?
OEDIPUS
Whate'er I utter, have no fear of me.
CHORUS
Begone!
OEDIPUS
            O wretched me!
CHORUS
                        Begone!
OEDIPUS
O daughter, what will hap anon?
CHORUS
Forth from our borders speed ye both!
OEDIPUS
How keep you then your troth?
CHORUS
Heaven's justice never smites
Him who ill with ill requites.
But if guile with guile contend,

Bane, not blessing, is the end.
Arise, begone and take thee hence straightway,
Lest on our land a heavier curse thou lay.
ANTIGONE
   O sirs! ye suffered not my father blind,
   Albeit gracious and to ruth inclined,
   Knowing the deeds he wrought, not innocent,
      But with no ill intent;
      Yet heed a maiden's moan
      Who pleads for him alone;
      My eyes, not reft of sight,
Plead with you as a daughter's might
You are our providence,
O make us not go hence!
O with a gracious nod
Grant us the nigh despaired-of boon we crave?
      Hear us, O hear,
But all that ye hold dear,
Wife, children, homestead, hearth and God!
Where will you find one, search ye ne'er so well.
Who 'scapes perdition if a god impel!
CHORUS
Surely we pity thee and him alike
Daughter of Oedipus, for your distress;
But as we reverence the decrees of Heaven
We cannot say aught other than we said.
OEDIPUS
O what avails renown or fair repute?
Are they not vanity? For, look you, now
Athens is held of States the most devout,
Athens alone gives hospitality
And shelters the vexed stranger, so men say.
Have I found so? I whom ye dislodged
First from my seat of rock and now would drive
Forth from your land, dreading my name alone;
For me you surely dread not, nor my deeds,
Deeds of a man more sinned against than sinning,
As I might well convince you, were it meet
To tell my mother's story and my sire's,
The cause of this your fear. Yet am I then
A villain born because in self-defense,
Striken, I struck the striker back again?
E'en had I known, no villainy 'twould prove:
But all unwitting whither I went, I went—
To ruin; my destroyers knew it well,
Wherefore, I pray you, sirs, in Heaven's name,
Even as ye bade me quit my seat, defend me.
O pay not a lip service to the gods
And wrong them of their dues. Bethink ye well,
The eye of Heaven beholds the just of men,
And the unjust, nor ever in this world
Has one sole godless sinner found escape.
Stand then on Heaven's side and never blot
Athens' fair scutcheon by abetting wrong.
I came to you a suppliant, and you pledged
Your honor; O preserve me to the end,
O let not this marred visage do me wrong!
A holy and god-fearing man is here
Whose coming purports comfort for your folk.
And when your chief arrives, whoe'er he be,
Then shall ye have my story and know all.
Meanwhile I pray you do me no despite.

43

CHORUS
The plea thou urgest, needs must give us pause,
Set forth in weighty argument, but we
Must leave the issue with the ruling powers.
OEDIPUS
Where is he, strangers, he who sways the realm?
CHORUS
In his ancestral seat; a messenger,
The same who sent us here, is gone for him.
OEDIPUS
And think you he will have such care or thought
For the blind stranger as to come himself?
CHORUS
Aye, that he will, when once he learns thy name.
OEDIPUS
But who will bear him word!
CHORUS
                    The way is long,
And many travelers pass to speed the news.
Be sure he'll hear and hasten, never fear;
So wide and far thy name is noised abroad,
That, were he ne'er so spent and loth to move,
He would bestir him when he hears of thee.
OEDIPUS
Well, may he come with blessing to his State
And me! Who serves his neighbor serves himself. 5
ANTIGONE
Zeus! What is this? What can I say or think?
OEDIPUS
What now, Antigone?
ANTIGONE
                    I see a woman
Riding upon a colt of Aetna's breed;
She wears for headgear a Thessalian hat
To shade her from the sun. Who can it be?
She or a stranger? Do I wake or dream?
'This she; 'tis not—I cannot tell, alack;
It is no other! Now her bright'ning glance
Greets me with recognition, yes, 'tis she,
Herself, Ismene!
OEDIPUS
                    Ha! what say ye, child?
ANTIGONE
That I behold thy daughter and my sister,
And thou wilt know her straightway by her voice.
[Enter ISMENE]
ISMENE
Father and sister, names to me most sweet,
How hardly have I found you, hardly now
When found at last can see you through my tears!
OEDIPUS
Art come, my child?
ISMENE
                    O father, sad thy plight!
OEDIPUS
Child, thou art here?
ISMENE
                    Yes, 'twas a weary way.
OEDIPUS
Touch me, my child.
ISMENE
                    I give a hand to both.
OEDIPUS
O children—sisters!
ISMENE
                    O disastrous plight!
OEDIPUS
Her plight and mine?
ISMENE

44

Aye, and my own no less.

OEDIPUS

What brought thee, daughter?

ISMENE

Father, care for thee.

OEDIPUS

A daughter's yearning?

ISMENE

Yes, and I had news
I would myself deliver, so I came
With the one thrall who yet is true to me.

OEDIPUS

Thy valiant brothers, where are they at
need?

ISMENE

They are—enough, 'tis now their darkest
hour.

OEDIPUS

Out on the twain! The thoughts and
actions all
Are framed and modeled on Egyptian
ways.
For there the men sit at the loom indoors
While the wives slave abroad for daily
bread.
So you, my children—those whom I
behooved
To bear the burden, stay at home like
girls,
While in their stead my daughters moil
and drudge,
Lightening their father's misery. The
one
Since first she grew from girlish
feebleness
To womanhood has been the old man's
guide
And shared my weary wandering,
roaming oft
Hungry and footsore through wild forest
ways,
In drenching rains and under scorching
suns,
Careless herself of home and ease, if so
Her sire might have her tender ministry.

And thou, my child, whilom thou wentest
forth,
Eluding the Cadmeians' vigilance,
To bring thy father all the oracles
Concerning Oedipus, and didst make
thyself
My faithful lieger, when they banished
me.
And now what mission summons thee
from home,
What news, Ismene, hast thou for thy
father?
This much I know, thou com'st not
empty-handed,
Without a warning of some new alarm.

ISMENE

The toil and trouble, father, that I bore
To find thy lodging-place and how thou
faredst,
I spare thee; surely 'twere a double pain
To suffer, first in act and then in telling;
'Tis the misfortune of thine ill-starred
sons
I come to tell thee. At the first they
willed
To leave the throne to Creon, minded
well
Thus to remove the inveterate curse of
old,
A canker that infected all thy race.
But now some god and an infatuate soul
Have stirred betwixt them a mad rivalry
To grasp at sovereignty and kingly
power.
Today the hot-branded youth, the
younger born,
Is keeping Polyneices from the throne,
His elder, and has thrust him from the
land.
The banished brother (so all Thebes
reports)
Fled to the vale of Argos, and by help
Of new alliance there and friends in
arms,

Swears he will stablish Argos straight as lord
Of the Cadmeian land, or, if he fail,
Exalt the victor to the stars of heaven.
This is no empty tale, but deadly truth,
My father; and how long thy agony,
Ere the gods pity thee, I cannot tell.
OEDIPUS
Hast thou indeed then entertained a hope
The gods at last will turn and rescue me?
ISMENE
Yea, so I read these latest oracles.
OEDIPUS
What oracles? What hath been uttered, child?
ISMENE
Thy country (so it runs) shall yearn in time
To have thee for their weal alive or dead.
OEDIPUS
And who could gain by such a one as I?
ISMENE
On thee, 'tis said, their sovereignty depends.
OEDIPUS
So, when I cease to be, my worth begins.
ISMENE
The gods, who once abased, uplift thee now.
OEDIPUS
Poor help to raise an old man fallen in youth.
ISMENE
Howe'er that be, 'tis for this cause alone
That Creon comes to thee—and comes anon.
OEDIPUS
With what intent, my daughter? Tell me plainly.
ISMENE
To plant thee near the Theban land, and so
Keep thee within their grasp, yet now allow

Thy foot to pass beyond their boundaries.
OEDIPUS
What gain they, if I lay outside?
OEDIPUS
                              Thy tomb,
If disappointed, brings on them a curse.
OEDIPUS
It needs no god to tell what's plain to sense.
ISMENE
Therefore they fain would have thee close at hand,
Not where thou wouldst be master of thyself.
OEDIPUS
Mean they to shroud my bones in Theban dust?
ISMENE
Nay, father, guilt of kinsman's blood forbids.
OEDIPUS
Then never shall they be my masters, never!
ISMENE
Thebes, thou shalt rue this bitterly some day!
OEDIPUS
When what conjunction comes to pass, my child?
ISMENE
Thy angry wraith, when at thy tomb they stand. 6
OEDIPUS
And who hath told thee what thou tell'st me, child?
ISMENE
Envoys who visited the Delphic hearth.
OEDIPUS
Hath Phoebus spoken thus concerning me?
ISMENE
So say the envoys who returned to Thebes.
OEDIPUS

And can a son of mine have heard of
this?
ISMENE
Yea, both alike, and know its import well.
OEDIPUS
They knew it, yet the ignoble greed of
rule
Outweighed all longing for their sire's
return.
ISMENE
Grievous thy words, yet I must own
them true.
OEDIPUS
Then may the gods ne'er quench their
fatal feud,
And mine be the arbitrament of the fight,
For which they now are arming, spear to
spear;
That neither he who holds the scepter
now
May keep this throne, nor he who fled
the realm
Return again. They never raised a hand,
When I their sire was thrust from hearth
and home,
When I was banned and banished, what
recked they?
Say you 'twas done at my desire, a grace
Which the state, yielding to my wish,
allowed?
Not so; for, mark you, on that very day
When in the tempest of my soul I craved
Death, even death by stoning, none
appeared
To further that wild longing, but anon,
When time had numbed my anguish and
I felt
My wrath had all outrun those errors
past,
Then, then it was the city went about
By force to oust me, respited for years;
And then my sons, who should as sons
have helped,
Did nothing: and, one little word from
them

Was all I needed, and they spoke no
word,
But let me wander on for evermore,
A banished man, a beggar. These two
maids
Their sisters, girls, gave all their sex
could give,
Food and safe harborage and filial care;
While their two brethren sacrificed their
sire
For lust of power and sceptred
sovereignty.
No! me they ne'er shall win for an ally,
Nor will this Theban kingship bring
them gain;
That know I from this maiden's oracles,
And those old prophecies concerning
me,
Which Phoebus now at length has
brought to pass.
Come Creon then, come all the mightiest
In Thebes to seek me; for if ye my
friends,
Championed by those dread Powers
indigenous,
Espouse my cause; then for the State ye
gain
A great deliverer, for my foemen bane.
CHORUS
Our pity, Oedipus, thou needs must
move,
Thou and these maidens; and the
stronger plea
Thou urgest, as the savior of our land,
Disposes me to counsel for thy weal.
OEDIPUS
Aid me, kind sirs; I will do all you bid.
CHORUS
First make atonement to the deities,
Whose grove by trespass thou didst first
profane.
OEDIPUS
After what manner, stranger? Teach me,
pray.
CHORUS

Make a libation first of water fetched
With undefiled hands from living spring.
OEDIPUS
And after I have gotten this pure
draught?
CHORUS
Bowls thou wilt find, the carver's
handiwork;
Crown thou the rims and both the
handles crown—
OEDIPUS
With olive shoots or blocks of wool, or
how?
CHORUS
With wool from fleece of yearling freshly
shorn.
OEDIPUS
What next? how must I end the ritual?
CHORUS
Pour thy libation, turning to the dawn.
OEDIPUS
Pouring it from the urns whereof ye
spake?
CHORUS
Yea, in three streams; and be the last
bowl drained
To the last drop.
OEDIPUS
       And wherewith shall I fill it,
Ere in its place I set it? This too tell.
CHORUS
With water and with honey; add no
wine.
OEDIPUS
And when the embowered earth hath
drunk thereof?
CHORUS
Then lay upon it thrice nine olive sprays
With both thy hands, and offer up this
prayer.
OEDIPUS
I fain would hear it; that imports the
most.
CHORUS

That, as we call them Gracious, they
would deign
To grant the suppliant their saving grace
So pray thyself or whoso pray for thee,
In whispered accents, not with lifted
voice;
Then go and look back. Do as I bid,
And I shall then be bold to stand thy
friend;
Else, stranger, I should have my fears for
thee.
OEDIPUS
Hear ye, my daughters, what these
strangers say?
ANTIGONE
We listened, and attend thy bidding,
father.
OEDIPUS
I cannot go, disabled as I am
Doubly, by lack of strength and lack of
sight;
But one of you may do it in my stead;
For one, I trow, may pay the sacrifice
Of thousands, if his heart be leal and
true.
So to your work with speed, but leave
me not
Untended; for this frame is all too week
To move without the help of guiding
hand.
ISMENE
Then I will go perform these rites, but
where
To find the spot, this have I yet to learn.
CHORUS
Beyond this grove; if thou hast need of
aught,
The guardian of the close will lend his
aid.
ISMENE
I go, and thou, Antigone, meanwhile
Must guard our father. In a parent's
cause
Toil, if there be toil, is of no account.
[Exit ISMENE]

48

CHORUS
(Str. 1)
Ill it is, stranger, to awake
Pain that long since has ceased to ache,
And yet I fain would hear—
OEDIPUS
What thing?
CHORUS
Thy tale of cruel suffering
For which no cure was found,
The fate that held thee bound.
OEDIPUS
O bid me not (as guest I claim
This grace) expose my shame.
CHORUS
The tale is bruited far and near,
And echoes still from ear to ear.
The truth, I fain would hear.
OEDIPUS
Ah me!
CHORUS
   I prithee yield.
OEDIPUS
      Ah me!
CHORUS
Grant my request, I granted all to thee.
OEDIPUS
(Ant. 1)
Know then I suffered ills most vile, but none
(So help me Heaven!) from acts in malice done.
CHORUS
Say how.
OEDIPUS
   The State around
An all unwitting bridegroom bound
An impious marriage chain;
   That was my bane.
CHORUS
Didst thou in sooth then share
A bed incestuous with her that bare—
OEDIPUS
It stabs me like a sword,
That two-edged word,

O stranger, but these maids—my own—
CHORUS
Say on.
OEDIPUS
Two daughters, curses twain.
CHORUS
Oh God!
OEDIPUS
Sprang from the wife and mother's travail-pain.
CHORUS
(Str. 2)
What, then thy offspring are at once—
OEDIPUS
      Too true.
Their father's very sister's too.
CHORUS
Oh horror!
OEDIPUS
   Horrors from the boundless deep
Back on my soul in refluent surges sweep.
CHORUS
Thou hast endured—
OEDIPUS
   Intolerable woe.
CHORUS
And sinned—
OEDIPUS
   I sinned not.
CHORUS
     How so?
OEDIPUS
I served the State; would I had never won
That graceless grace by which I was undone.
CHORUS
(Ant. 2)
And next, unhappy man, thou hast shed blood?
OEDIPUS
Must ye hear more?
CHORUS
   A father's?

OEDIPUS
                    Flood on flood
Whelms me; that word's a second mortal
blow.
CHORUS
Murderer!
OEDIPUS
            Yes, a murderer, but know—
CHORUS
What canst thou plead?
OEDIPUS
                    A plea of justice.
CHORUS
                            How?
OEDIPUS
I slew who else would me have slain;
I slew without intent,
A wretch, but innocent
In the law's eye, I stand, without a stain.
CHORUS
Behold our sovereign, Theseus, Aegeus'
son,
Comes at thy summons to perform his
part.
[Enter THESEUS]
THESEUS
Oft had I heard of thee in times gone
by—
The bloody mutilation of thine eyes—
And therefore know thee, son of Laius.
All that I lately gathered on the way
Made my conjecture doubly sure; and
now
Thy garb and that marred visage prove
to me
That thou art he. So pitying thine estate,
Most ill-starred Oedipus, I fain would
know
What is the suit ye urge on me and
Athens,
Thou and the helpless maiden at thy
side.
Declare it; dire indeed must be the tale
Whereat I should recoil. I too was
reared,

Like thee, in exile, and in foreign lands
Wrestled with many perils, no man
more.
Wherefore no alien in adversity
Shall seek in vain my succor, nor shalt
thou;
I know myself a mortal, and my share
In what the morrow brings no more than
thine.
OEDIPUS
Theseus, thy words so apt, so generous
So comfortable, need no long reply
Both who I am and of what lineage
sprung,
And from what land I came, thou hast
declared.
So without prologue I may utter now
My brief petition, and the tale is told.
THESEUS
Say on, and tell me what I fain would
learn.
OEDIPUS
I come to offer thee this woe-worn
frame,
A gift not fair to look on; yet its worth
More precious far than any outward
show.
THESEUS
What profit dost thou proffer to have
brought?
OEDIPUS
Hereafter thou shalt learn, not yet,
methinks.
THESEUS
When may we hope to reap the benefit?
OEDIPUS
When I am dead and thou hast buried
me.
THESEUS
Thou cravest life's last service; all
before—
Is it forgotten or of no account?
OEDIPUS
Yea, the last boon is warrant for the rest.
THESEUS

The grace thou cravest then is small indeed.

OEDIPUS
Nay, weigh it well; the issue is not slight.

THESEUS
Thou meanest that betwixt thy sons and me?

OEDIPUS
Prince, they would fain convey me back to Thebes.

THESEUS
If there be no compulsion, then methinks
To rest in banishment befits not thee.

OEDIPUS
Nay, when I wished it they would not consent.

THESEUS
For shame! such temper misbecomes the faller.

OEDIPUS
Chide if thou wilt, but first attend my plea.

THESEUS
Say on, I wait full knowledge ere I judge.

OEDIPUS
O Theseus, I have suffered wrongs on wrongs.

THESEUS
Wouldst tell the old misfortune of thy race?

OEDIPUS
No, that has grown a byword throughout Greece.

THESEUS
What then can be this more than mortal grief?

OEDIPUS
My case stands thus; by my own flesh and blood
I was expelled my country, and can ne'er
Thither return again, a parricide.

THESEUS
Why fetch thee home if thou must needs obey.

THESEUS
What are they threatened by the oracle?

OEDIPUS
Destruction that awaits them in this land.

THESEUS
What can beget ill blood 'twixt them and me?

OEDIPUS
Dear son of Aegeus, to the gods alone
Is given immunity from eld and death;
But nothing else escapes all-ruinous time.
Earth's might decays, the might of men decays,
Honor grows cold, dishonor flourishes,
There is no constancy 'twixt friend and friend,
Or city and city; be it soon or late,
Sweet turns to bitter, hate once more to love.
If now 'tis sunshine betwixt Thebes and thee
And not a cloud, Time in his endless course
Gives birth to endless days and nights, wherein
The merest nothing shall suffice to cut
With serried spears your bonds of amity.
Then shall my slumbering and buried corpse
In its cold grave drink their warm life-blood up,
If Zeus be Zeus and Phoebus still speak true.
No more: 'tis ill to tear aside the veil
Of mysteries; let me cease as I began:
Enough if thou wilt keep thy plighted troth,
Then shall thou ne'er complain that Oedipus
Proved an unprofitable and thankless guest,
Except the gods themselves shall play me false.

CHORUS

51

The man, my lord, has from the very first
Declared his power to offer to our land
These and like benefits.
THESEUS
Who could reject
The proffered amity of such a friend?
First, he can claim the hospitality
To which by mutual contract we stand
pledged:
Next, coming here, a suppliant to the
gods,
He pays full tribute to the State and me;
His favors therefore never will I spurn,
But grant him the full rights of citizen;
And, if it suits the stranger here to bide,
I place him in your charge, or if he please
Rather to come with me—choose,
Oedipus,
Which of the two thou wilt. Thy choice is
mine.
OEDIPUS
Zeus, may the blessing fall on men like
these!
THESEUS
What dost thou then decide—to come
with me?
OEDIPUS
Yea, were it lawful—but 'tis rather
here—
THESEUS
What wouldst thou here? I shall not
thwart thy wish.
OEDIPUS
Here shall I vanquish those who cast me
forth.
THESEUS
Then were thy presence here a boon
indeed.
OEDIPUS
Such shall it prove, if thou fulfill'st thy
pledge.
THESEUS
Fear not for me; I shall not play thee
false.
OEDIPUS

No need to back thy promise with an
oath.
THESEUS
An oath would be no surer than my
word.
OEDIPUS
How wilt thou act then?
THESEUS
What is it thou fear'st?
OEDIPUS
My foes will come—
THESEUS
Our friends will look to that.
OEDIPUS
But if thou leave me?
THESEUS
Teach me not my duty.
OEDIPUS
'Tis fear constrains me.
THESEUS
My soul knows no fear!
OEDIPUS
Thou knowest not what threats—
THESEUS
I know that none
Shall hale thee hence in my despite.
Such threats
Vented in anger oft, are blusterers,
An idle breath, forgot when sense
returns.
And for thy foemen, though their words
were brave,
Boasting to bring thee back, they are like
to find
The seas between us wide and hard to
sail.
Such my firm purpose, but in any case
Take heart, since Phoebus sent thee
here. My name,
Though I be distant, warrants thee from
harm.
CHORUS
(Str. 1)
Thou hast come to a steed-famed land
for rest,

52

O stranger worn with toil,
To a land of all lands the goodliest
    Colonus' glistening soil.
'Tis the haunt of the clear-voiced
nightingale,
    Who hid in her bower, among
The wine-dark ivy that wreathes the
vale,
    Trilleth her ceaseless song;
And she loves, where the clustering
berries nod
    O'er a sunless, windless glade,
The spot by no mortal footstep trod,
The pleasance kept for the Bacchic
god,
Where he holds each night his revels
wild
With the nymphs who fostered the
lusty child.
(Ant. 1)
    And fed each morn by the pearly dew
        The starred narcissi shine,
    And a wreath with the crocus' golden
hue
        For the Mother and Daughter
twine.
    And never the sleepless fountains
cease
        That feed Cephisus' stream,
    But they swell earth's bosom with
quick increase,
        And their wave hath a crystal
gleam.
    And the Muses' quire will never
disdain
    To visit this heaven-favored plain,
    Nor the Cyprian queen of the golden
rein.
(Str. 2)
    And here there grows, unpruned,
untamed,
        Terror to foemen's spear,
    A tree in Asian soil unnamed,
    By Pelops' Dorian isle unclaimed,
        Self-nurtured year by year;

'Tis the grey-leaved olive that feeds
our boys;
    Nor youth nor withering age destroys
    The plant that the Olive Planter tends
    And the Grey-eyed Goddess herself
defends.
(Ant. 2)
    Yet another gift, of all gifts the most
    Prized by our fatherland, we boast—
    The might of the horse, the might of
the sea;
    Our fame, Poseidon, we owe to thee,
    Son of Kronos, our king divine,
    Who in these highways first didst fit
    For the mouth of horses the iron bit;
    Thou too hast taught us to fashion
meet
    For the arm of the rower the oar-
blade fleet,
        Swift as the Nereids' hundred feet
    As they dance along the brine.
ANTIGONE
Oh land extolled above all lands, 'tis now
For thee to make these glorious titles
good.
OEDIPUS
Why this appeal, my daughter?
ANTIGONE
                Father, lo!
Creon approaches with his company.
OEDIPUS
Fear not, it shall be so; if we are old,
This country's vigor has no touch of age.
[Enter CREON with attendants]
CREON
Burghers, my noble friends, ye take
alarm
At my approach (I read it in your eyes),
Fear nothing and refrain from angry
words.
I come with no ill purpose; I am old,
And know the city whither I am come,
Without a peer amongst the powers of
Greece.
It was by reason of my years that I

Was chosen to persuade your guest and bring
Him back to Thebes; not the delegate
Of one man, but commissioned by the State,
Since of all Thebans I have most bewailed,
Being his kinsman, his most grievous woes.
O listen to me, luckless Oedipus,
Come home! The whole Cadmeian people claim
With right to have thee back, I most of all,
For most of all (else were I vile indeed)
I mourn for thy misfortunes, seeing thee
An aged outcast, wandering on and on,
A beggar with one handmaid for thy stay.
Ah! who had e'er imagined she could fall
To such a depth of misery as this,
To tend in penury thy stricken frame,
A virgin ripe for wedlock, but unwed,
A prey for any wanton ravisher?
Seems it not cruel this reproach I cast
On thee and on myself and all the race?
Aye, but an open shame cannot be hid.
Hide it, O hide it, Oedipus, thou canst.
O, by our fathers' gods, consent I pray;
Come back to Thebes, come to thy father's home,
Bid Athens, as is meet, a fond farewell;
Thebes thy old foster-mother claims thee first.

OEDIPUS
O front of brass, thy subtle tongue would twist
To thy advantage every plea of right
Why try thy arts on me, why spread again
Toils where 'twould gall me sorest to be snared?
In old days when by self-wrought woes distraught,
I yearned for exile as a glad release,
Thy will refused the favor then I craved.
But when my frenzied grief had spent its force,
And I was fain to taste the sweets of home,
Then thou wouldst thrust me from my country, then
These ties of kindred were by thee ignored;
And now again when thou behold'st this State
And all its kindly people welcome me,
Thou seek'st to part us, wrapping in soft words
Hard thoughts. And yet what pleasure canst thou find
In forcing friendship on unwilling foes?
Suppose a man refused to grant some boon
When you importuned him, and afterwards
When you had got your heart's desire, consented,
Granting a grace from which all grace had fled,
Would not such favor seem an empty boon?
Yet such the boon thou profferest now to me,
Fair in appearance, but when tested false.
Yea, I will proved thee false, that these may hear;
Thou art come to take me, not to take me home,
But plant me on thy borders, that thy State
May so escape annoyance from this land.
That thou shalt never gain, but this instead—
My ghost to haunt thy country without end;
And for my sons, this heritage—no more—
Just room to die in. Have not I more skill

54

Than thou to draw the horoscope of Thebes?
Are not my teachers surer guides than thine—
Great Phoebus and the sire of Phoebus, Zeus?
Thou art a messenger suborned, thy tongue
Is sharper than a sword's edge, yet thy speech
Will bring thee more defeats than victories.
Howbeit, I know I waste my words—begone,
And leave me here; whate'er may be my lot,
He lives not ill who lives withal content.

CREON
Which loses in this parley, I o'erthrown
By thee, or thou who overthrow'st thyself?

OEDIPUS
I shall be well contented if thy suit
Fails with these strangers, as it has with me.

CREON
Unhappy man, will years ne'er make thee wise?
Must thou live on to cast a slur on age?

OEDIPUS
Thou hast a glib tongue, but no honest man,
Methinks, can argue well on any side.

CREON
'Tis one thing to speak much, another well.

OEDIPUS
Thy words, forsooth, are few and all well aimed!

CREON
Not for a man indeed with wits like thine.

OEDIPUS
Depart! I bid thee in these burghers' name,
And prowl no longer round me to blockade
My destined harbor.

CREON
          I protest to these,
Not thee, and for thine answer to thy kin,
If e'er I take thee—

OEDIPUS
          Who against their will
Could take me?

CREON
          Though untaken thou shalt smart.

OEDIPUS
What power hast thou to execute this threat?

CREON
One of thy daughters is already seized,
The other I will carry off anon.

OEDIPUS
Woe, woe!

CREON
          This is but prelude to thy woes.

OEDIPUS
Hast thou my child?

CREON
          And soon shall have the other.

OEDIPUS
Ho, friends! ye will not surely play me false?
Chase this ungodly villain from your land.

CHORUS
Hence, stranger, hence avaunt! Thou doest wrong
In this, and wrong in all that thou hast done.

CREON (to his guards)
'Tis time by force to carry off the girl,
If she refuse of her free will to go.

ANTIGONE
Ah, woe is me! where shall I fly, where find
Succor from gods or men?

CHORUS

What would'st thou,
stranger?
CREON
I meddle not with him, but her who is
mine.
OEDIPUS
O princes of the land!
CHORUS
           Sir, thou dost wrong.
CREON
Nay, right.
CHORUS
      How right?
CREON
           I take but what is mine.
OEDIPUS
Help, Athens!
CHORUS
What means this, sirrah? quick unhand
her, or
We'll fight it out.
CREON
        Back!
CHORUS
          Not till thou forbear.
CREON
'Tis war with Thebes if I am touched or
harmed.
OEDIPUS
Did I not warn thee?
CHORUS
        Quick, unhand the maid!
CREON
Command your minions; I am not your
slave.
CHORUS
Desist, I bid thee.
CREON (to the guard)
        And O bid thee march!
CHORUS
    To the rescue, one and all!
    Rally, neighbors to my call!
    See, the foe is at the gate!
    Rally to defend the State.
ANTIGONE

Ah, woe is me, they drag me hence, O
friends.
OEDIPUS
Where art thou, daughter?
ANTIGONE
        Haled along by force.
OEDIPUS
Thy hands, my child!
ANTIGONE
      They will not let me, father.
CREON
Away with her!
OEDIPUS
      Ah, woe is me, ah woe!
CREON
So those two crutches shall no longer
serve thee
For further roaming. Since it pleaseth
thee
To triumph o'er thy country and thy
friends
Who mandate, though a prince, I here
discharge,
Enjoy thy triumph; soon or late thou'lt
find
Thou art an enemy to thyself, both now
And in time past, when in despite of
friends
Thou gav'st the rein to passion, still thy
bane.
CHORUS
Hold there, sir stranger!
CREON
      Hands off, have a care.
CHORUS
Restore the maidens, else thou goest not.
CREON
Then Thebes will take a dearer surety
soon;
I will lay hands on more than these two
maids.
CHORUS
What canst thou further?
CREON
      Carry off this man.

CHORUS
Brave words!
CREON
     And deeds forthwith shall make them good.
CHORUS
Unless perchance our sovereign intervene.
OEDIPUS
O shameless voice! Would'st lay an hand on me?
CREON
Silence, I bid thee!
OEDIPUS
     Goddesses, allow
Thy suppliant to utter yet one curse!
Wretch, now my eyes are gone thou hast torn away
The helpless maiden who was eyes to me;
For these to thee and all thy cursed race
May the great Sun, whose eye is everywhere,
Grant length of days and old age like to mine.
CREON
Listen, O men of Athens, mark ye this?
OEDIPUS
They mark us both and understand that I
Wronged by the deeds defend myself with words.
CREON
Nothing shall curb my will; though I be old
And single-handed, I will have this man.
OEDIPUS
O woe is me!
CHORUS
Thou art a bold man, stranger, if thou think'st
To execute thy purpose.
CREON
     So I do.
CHORUS

Then shall I deem this State no more a State.
CREON
With a just quarrel weakness conquers might.
OEDIPUS
Ye hear his words?
CHORUS
     Aye words, but not yet deeds,
Zeus knoweth!
CREON
     Zeus may haply know, not thou.
CHORUS
Insolence!
CREON
     Insolence that thou must bear.
CHORUS
     Haste ye princes, sound the alarm!
     Men of Athens, arm ye, arm!
     Quickly to the rescue come
     Ere the robbers get them home.
[Enter THESEUS]
THESEUS
Why this outcry? What is forward? wherefore was I called away
From the altar of Poseidon, lord of your Colonus? Say!
On what errand have I hurried hither without stop or stay.
OEDIPUS
Dear friend—those accents tell me who thou art—
Yon man but now hath done me a foul wrong.
THESEUS
What is this wrong and who hath wrought it? Speak.
OEDIPUS
Creon who stands before thee. He it is
Hath robbed me of my all, my daughters twain.
THESEUS
What means this?
OEDIPUS

Thou hast heard my tale of wrongs.

THESEUS
Ho! hasten to the altars, one of you.
Command my liegemen leave the sacrifice
And hurry, foot and horse, with rein unchecked,
To where the paths that packmen use diverge,
Lest the two maidens slip away, and I
Become a mockery to this my guest,
As one despoiled by force. Quick, as I bid.
As for this stranger, had I let my rage,
Justly provoked, have play, he had not 'scaped
Scathless and uncorrected at my hands.
But now the laws to which himself appealed,
These and none others shall adjudicate.
Thou shalt not quit this land, till thou hast fetched
The maidens and produced them in my sight.
Thou hast offended both against myself
And thine own race and country. Having come
Unto a State that champions right and asks
For every action warranty of law,
Thou hast set aside the custom of the land,
And like some freebooter art carrying off
What plunder pleases thee, as if forsooth
Thou thoughtest this a city without men,
Or manned by slaves, and me a thing of naught.
Yet not from Thebes this villainy was learnt;
Thebes is not wont to breed unrighteous sons,
Nor would she praise thee, if she learnt that thou

Wert robbing me—aye and the gods to boot,
Haling by force their suppliants, poor maids.
Were I on Theban soil, to prosecute
The justest claim imaginable, I
Would never wrest by violence my own
Without sanction of your State or King;
I should behave as fits an outlander
Living amongst a foreign folk, but thou
Shamest a city that deserves it not,
Even thine own, and plentitude of years
Have made of thee an old man and a fool.
Therefore again I charge thee as before,
See that the maidens are restored at once,
Unless thou would'st continue here by force
And not by choice a sojourner; so much
I tell thee home and what I say, I mean.

CHORUS
Thy case is perilous; though by birth and race
Thou should'st be just, thou plainly doest wrong.

CREON
Not deeming this city void of men
Or counsel, son of Aegeus, as thou say'st
I did what I have done; rather I thought
Your people were not like to set such store
by kin of mine and keep them 'gainst my will.
Nor would they harbor, so I stood assured,
A godless parricide, a reprobate
Convicted of incestuous marriage ties.
For on her native hill of Ares here
(I knew your far-famed Areopagus)
Sits Justice, and permits not vagrant folk
To stay within your borders. In that faith
I hunted down my quarry; and e'en then
I had refrained but for the curses dire

Wherewith he banned my kinsfolk and myself:
Such wrong, methought, had warrant for my act.
Anger has no old age but only death;
The dead alone can feel no touch of spite.
So thou must work thy will; my cause is just
But weak without allies; yet will I try,
Old as I am, to answer deeds with deeds.
OEDIPUS
O shameless railer, think'st thou this abuse
Defames my grey hairs rather than thine own?
Murder and incest, deeds of horror, all
Thou blurtest forth against me, all I have borne,
No willing sinner; so it pleased the gods
Wrath haply with my sinful race of old,
Since thou could'st find no sin in me myself
For which in retribution I was doomed
To trespass thus against myself and mine.
Answer me now, if by some oracle
My sire was destined to a bloody end
By a son's hand, can this reflect on me,
Me then unborn, begotten by no sire,
Conceived in no mother's womb? And if
When born to misery, as born I was,
I met my sire, not knowing whom I met or what I did, and slew him, how canst thou
With justice blame the all-unconscious hand?
And for my mother, wretch, art not ashamed,
Seeing she was thy sister, to extort
From me the story of her marriage, such
A marriage as I straightway will proclaim.
For I will speak; thy lewd and impious speech
Has broken all the bonds of reticence.

She was, ah woe is me! she was my mother;
I knew it not, nor she; and she my mother
Bare children to the son whom she had borne,
A birth of shame. But this at least I know
Wittingly thou aspersest her and me;
But I unwitting wed, unwilling speak.
Nay neither in this marriage or this deed
Which thou art ever casting in my teeth—
A murdered sire—shall I be held to blame.
Come, answer me one question, if thou canst:
If one should presently attempt thy life,
Would'st thou, O man of justice, first inquire
If the assassin was perchance thy sire,
Or turn upon him? As thou lov'st thy life,
On thy aggressor thou would'st turn, no stay
Debating, if the law would bear thee out.
Such was my case, and such the pass whereto
The gods reduced me; and methinks my sire,
Could he come back to life, would not dissent.
Yet thou, for just thou art not, but a man
Who sticks at nothing, if it serve his plea,
Reproachest me with this before these men.
It serves thy turn to laud great Theseus' name,
And Athens as a wisely governed State;
Yet in thy flatteries one thing is to seek:
If any land knows how to pay the gods
Their proper rites, 'tis Athens most of all.
This is the land whence thou wast fain to steal
Their aged suppliant and hast carried off
My daughters. Therefore to yon goddesses,

I turn, adjure them and invoke their aid
To champion my cause, that thou mayest learn
What is the breed of men who guard this State.
CHORUS
An honest man, my liege, one sore bestead
By fortune, and so worthy our support.
THESEUS
Enough of words; the captors speed amain,
While we the victims stand debating here.
CREON
What would'st thou? What can I, a feeble man?
THESEUS
Show us the trail, and I'll attend thee too,
That, if thou hast the maidens hereabouts,
Thou mayest thyself discover them to me;
But if thy guards outstrip us with their spoil,
We may draw rein; for others speed, from whom
They will not 'scape to thank the gods at home.
Lead on, I say, the captor's caught, and fate
Hath ta'en the fowler in the toils he spread;
So soon are lost gains gotten by deceit.
And look not for allies; I know indeed
Such height of insolence was never reached
Without abettors or accomplices;
Thou hast some backer in thy bold essay,
But I will search this matter home and see
One man doth not prevail against the State.
Dost take my drift, or seem these words as vain

As seemed our warnings when the plot was hatched?
CREON
Nothing thou sayest can I here dispute,
But once at home I too shall act my part.
THESEUS
Threaten us and—begone! Thou, Oedipus,
Stay here assured that nothing save my death
Will stay my purpose to restore the maids.
OEDIPUS
Heaven bless thee, Theseus, for thy nobleness
And all thy loving care in my behalf.
[Exeunt THESEUS and CREON]
CHORUS
(Str. 1)
 O when the flying foe,
 Turning at last to bay,
 Soon will give blow for blow,
 Might I behold the fray;
 Hear the loud battle roar
 Swell, on the Pythian shore,
 Or by the torch-lit bay,
 Where the dread Queen and Maid
 Cherish the mystic rites,
 Rites they to none betray,
 Ere on his lips is laid
 Secrecy's golden key
 By their own acolytes,
 Priestly Eumolpidae.
 There I might chance behold
 Theseus our captain bold
 Meet with the robber band,
 Ere they have fled the land,
 Rescue by might and main
 Maidens, the captives twain.
(Ant. 1)
 Haply on swiftest steed,
 Or in the flying car,
 Now they approach the glen,
 West of white Oea's scaur.
 They will be vanquished:

60

Dread are our warriors, dread
Theseus our chieftain's men.
Flashes each bridle bright,
Charges each gallant knight,
All that our Queen adore,
Pallas their patron, or
Him whose wide floods enring
Earth, the great Ocean-king
Whom Rhea bore.
(Str. 2)
Fight they or now prepare
To fight? a vision rare
Tells me that soon again
I shall behold the twain
Maidens so ill bestead,
By their kin buffeted.
Today, today Zeus worketh some great
thing
    This day shall victory bring.
O for the wings, the wings of a dove,
To be borne with the speed of the gale,
Up and still upwards to sail
    And gaze on the fray from the clouds
above.
(Ant. 2)
All-seeing Zeus, O lord of heaven,
To our guardian host be given
Might triumphant to surprise
Flying foes and win their prize.
Hear us, Zeus, and hear us, child
Of Zeus, Athene undefiled,
Hear, Apollo, hunter, hear,
Huntress, sister of Apollo,
Who the dappled swift-foot deer
O'er the wooded glade dost follow;
Help with your two-fold power
Athens in danger's hour!
O wayfarer, thou wilt not have to tax
The friends who watch for thee with
false presage,
For lo, an escort with the maids draws
near.
[Enter ANTIGONE and ISMENE with
THESEUS]
OEDIPUS

Where, where? what sayest thou?
ANTIGONE
                O father, father,
Would that some god might grant thee
eyes to see
This best of men who brings us back
again.
OEDIPUS
My child! and are ye back indeed!
ANTIGONE
                        Yes, saved
By Theseus and his gallant followers.
OEDIPUS
Come to your father's arms, O let me feel
A child's embrace I never hoped for
more.
ANTIGONE
Thou askest what is doubly sweet to
give.
OEDIPUS
Where are ye then?
ANTIGONE
            We come together both.
OEDIPUS
My precious nurslings!
ANTIGONE
            Fathers aye were fond.
OEDIPUS
Props of my age!
ANTIGONE
            So sorrow sorrow props.
OEDIPUS
I have my darlings, and if death should
come,
Death were not wholly bitter with you
near.
Cling to me, press me close on either
side,
There rest ye from your dreary
wayfaring.
Now tell me of your ventures, but in
brief;
Brief speech suffices for young maids
like you.
ANTIGONE

Here is our savior; thou should'st hear the tale
From his own lips; so shall my part be brief.
OEDIPUS
I pray thee do not wonder if the sight
Of children, given o'er for lost, has made
My converse somewhat long and tedious.
Full well I know the joy I have of them
Is due to thee, to thee and no man else;
Thou wast their sole deliverer, none else.
The gods deal with thee after my desire,
With thee and with this land! for fear of heaven
I found above all peoples most with you,
And righteousness and lips that cannot lie.
I speak in gratitude of what I know,
For all I have I owe to thee alone.
Give me thy hand, O Prince, that I may touch it,
And if thou wilt permit me, kiss thy cheek.
What say I? Can I wish that thou should'st touch
One fallen like me to utter wretchedness,
Corrupt and tainted with a thousand ills?
Oh no, I would not let thee if thou would'st.
They only who have known calamity
Can share it. Let me greet thee where thou art,
And still befriend me as thou hast till now.
THESEUS
I marvel not if thou hast dallied long
In converse with thy children and preferred
Their speech to mine; I feel no jealousy,
I would be famous more by deeds than words.
Of this, old friend, thou hast had proof; my oath

I have fulfilled and brought thee back the maids
Alive and nothing harmed for all those threats.
And how the fight was won, 'twere waste of words
To boast—thy daughters here will tell thee all.
But of a matter that has lately chanced
On my way hitherward, I fain would have
Thy counsel—slight 'twould seem, yet worthy thought.
A wise man heeds all matters great or small.
OEDIPUS
What is it, son of Aegeus? Let me hear.
Of what thou askest I myself know naught.
THESEUS
'Tis said a man, no countryman of thine,
But of thy kin, hath taken sanctuary
Beside the altar of Poseidon, where
I was at sacrifice when called away.
OEDIPUS
What is his country? what the suitor's prayer?
THESEUS
I know but one thing; he implores, I am told,
A word with thee—he will not trouble thee.
OEDIPUS
What seeks he? If a suppliant, something grave.
THESEUS
He only waits, they say, to speak with thee,
And then unharmed to go upon his way.
OEDIPUS
I marvel who is this petitioner.
THESEUS
Think if there be not any of thy kin
At Argos who might claim this boon of thee.

OEDIPUS
Dear friend, forbear, I pray.
THESEUS
                    What ails thee now?
OEDIPUS
Ask it not of me.
THESEUS
                    Ask not what? explain.
OEDIPUS
Thy words have told me who the
suppliant is.
THESEUS
Who can he be that I should frown on
him?
OEDIPUS
My son, O king, my hateful son, whose
words
Of all men's most would jar upon my
ears.
THESEUS
Thou sure mightest listen. If his suit
offend,
No need to grant it. Why so loth to hear
him?
OEDIPUS
That voice, O king, grates on a father's
ears;
I have come to loathe it. Force me not to
yield.
THESEUS
But he hath found asylum. O beware,
And fail not in due reverence to the god.
ANTIGONE
O heed me, father, though I am young in
years.
Let the prince have his will and pay
withal
What in his eyes is service to the god;
For our sake also let our brother come.
If what he urges tend not to thy good
He cannot surely wrest perforce thy will.
To hear him then, what harm? By open
words
A scheme of villainy is soon bewrayed.

Thou art his father, therefore canst not
pay
In kind a son's most impious outrages.
O listen to him; other men like thee
Have thankless children and are choleric,
But yielding to persuasion's gentle spell
They let their savage mood be exorcised.
Look thou to the past, forget the present,
think
On all the woe thy sire and mother
brought thee;
Thence wilt thou draw this lesson
without fail,
Of evil passion evil is the end.
Thou hast, alas, to prick thy memory,
Stern monitors, these ever-sightless
orbs.
O yield to us; just suitors should not
need
To be importunate, nor he that takes
A favor lack the grace to make return.
OEDIPUS
Grievous to me, my child, the boon ye
win
By pleading. Let it be then; have your
way
Only if come he must, I beg thee, friend,
Let none have power to dispose of me.
THESEUS
No need, Sir, to appeal a second time.
It likes me not to boast, but be assured
Thy life is safe while any god saves mine.
[Exit THESEUS]
CHORUS
(Str.)
Who craves excess of days,
            Scorning the common span
            Of life, I judge that man
A giddy wight who walks in folly's ways.
For the long years heap up a grievous
load,
            Scant pleasures, heavier pains,
            Till not one joy remains
For him who lingers on life's weary road
            And come it slow or fast,

63

One doom of fate
Doth all await,
For dance and marriage bell,
The dirge and funeral knell.
Death the deliverer freeth all at last.
(Ant.)
    Not to be born at all
    Is best, far best that can befall,
    Next best, when born, with least
delay
    To trace the backward way.
For when youth passes with its giddy
train,
    Troubles on troubles follow, toils on
toils,
    Pain, pain for ever pain;
    And none escapes life's coils.
    Envy, sedition, strife,
Carnage and war, make up the tale of
life.
Last comes the worst and most abhorred
stage
    Of unregarded age,
Joyless, companionless and slow,
    Of woes the crowning woe.
(Epode)
Such ills not I alone,
He too our guest hath known,
E'en as some headland on an iron-bound
shore,
Lashed by the wintry blasts and surge's
roar,
So is he buffeted on every side
By drear misfortune's whelming tide,
    By every wind of heaven o'erborne
    Some from the sunset, some from
orient morn,
    Some from the noonday glow.
Some from Rhipean gloom of everlasting
snow.
ANTIGONE
Father, methinks I see the stranger
coming,
Alone he comes and weeping plenteous
tears.

OEDIPUS
Who may he be?
ANTIGONE
    The same that we surmised.
From the outset—Polyneices. He is here.
[Enter POLYNEICES]
POLYNEICES
Ah me, my sisters, shall I first lament
My own afflictions, or my aged sire's,
Whom here I find a castaway, with you,
In a strange land, an ancient beggar clad
In antic tatters, marring all his frame,
While o'er the sightless orbs his unkept
locks
Float in the breeze; and, as it were to
match,
He bears a wallet against hunger's pinch.
All this too late I learn, wretch that I am,
Alas! I own it, and am proved most vile
In my neglect of thee: I scorn myself.
But as almighty Zeus in all he doth
Hath Mercy for co-partner of this throne,
Let Mercy, father, also sit enthroned
In thy heart likewise. For transgressions
past
May be amended, cannot be made worse.

Why silent? Father, speak, nor turn
away,
Hast thou no word, wilt thou dismiss me
then
In mute disdain, nor tell me why thou art
wrath?
O ye his daughters, sisters mine, do ye
This sullen, obstinate silence try to
move.
Let him not spurn, without a single word
Of answer, me the suppliant of the god.
ANTIGONE
Tell him thyself, unhappy one, thine
errand;
For large discourse may send a thrill of
joy,
Or stir a chord of wrath or tenderness,

64

And to the tongue-tied somehow give a tongue.
POLYNEICES
Well dost thou counsel, and I will speak out.
First will I call in aid the god himself,
Poseidon, from whose altar I was raised,
With warrant from the monarch of this land,
To parley with you, and depart unscathed.
These pledges, strangers, I would see observed
By you and by my sisters and my sire.
Now, father, let me tell thee why I came.
I have been banished from my native land
Because by right of primogeniture
I claimed possession of thy sovereign throne
Wherefrom Etocles, my younger brother,
Ousted me, not by weight of precedent,
Nor by the last arbitrament of war,
But by his popular acts; and the prime cause
Of this I deem the curse that rests on thee.
So likewise hold the soothsayers, for when
I came to Argos in the Dorian land
And took the king Adrastus' child to wife,
Under my standard I enlisted all
The foremost captains of the Apian isle,
To levy with their aid that sevenfold host
Of spearmen against Thebes, determining
To oust my foes or die in a just cause.
Why then, thou askest, am I here today?
Father, I come a suppliant to thee
Both for myself and my allies who now
With squadrons seven beneath their seven spears
Beleaguer all the plain that circles Thebes.
Foremost the peerless warrior, peerless seer,
Amphiaraiis with his lightning lance;
Next an Aetolian, Tydeus, Oeneus' son;
Eteoclus of Argive birth the third;
The fourth Hippomedon, sent to the war
By his sire Talaos; Capaneus, the fifth,
Vaunts he will fire and raze the town; the sixth
Parthenopaeus, an Arcadian born
Named of that maid, longtime a maid and late
Espoused, Atalanta's true-born child;
Last I thy son, or thine at least in name,
If but the bastard of an evil fate,
Lead against Thebes the fearless Argive host.
Thus by thy children and thy life, my sire,
We all adjure thee to remit thy wrath
And favor one who seeks a just revenge
Against a brother who has banned and robbed him.
For victory, if oracles speak true,
Will fall to those who have thee for ally.
So, by our fountains and familiar gods
I pray thee, yield and hear; a beggar I
And exile, thou an exile likewise; both
Involved in one misfortune find a home
As pensioners, while he, the lord of Thebes,
O agony! makes a mock of thee and me.
I'll scatter with a breath the upstart's might,
And bring thee home again and stablish thee,
And stablish, having cast him out, myself.
This will thy goodwill I will undertake,
Without it I can scare return alive.
CHORUS
For the king's sake who sent him, Oedipus,
Dismiss him not without a meet reply.
OEDIPUS

65

Nay, worthy seniors, but for Theseus'
sake
Who sent him hither to have word of me.
Never again would he have heard my
voice;
But now he shall obtain this parting
grace,
An answer that will bring him little joy.
O villain, when thou hadst the
sovereignty
That now thy brother holdeth in thy
stead,
Didst thou not drive me, thine own
father, out,
An exile, cityless, and make we wear
This beggar's garb thou weepest to
behold,
Now thou art come thyself to my sad
plight?
Nothing is here for tears; it must be
borne
By me till death, and I shall think of thee
As of my murderer; thou didst thrust me
out;
'Tis thou hast made me conversant with
woe,
Through thee I beg my bread in a
strange land;
And had not these my daughters tended
me
I had been dead for aught of aid from
thee.
They tend me, they preserve me, they
are men
Not women in true service to their sire;
But ye are bastards, and no sons of mine.
Therefore just Heaven hath an eye on
thee;
Howbeit not yet with aspect so austere
As thou shalt soon experience, if indeed
These banded hosts are moving against
Thebes.
That city thou canst never storm, but
first

Shall fall, thou and thy brother, blood-
imbrued.
Such curse I lately launched against you
twain,
Such curse I now invoke to fight for me,
That ye may learn to honor those who
bear thee
Nor flout a sightless father who begat
Degenerate sons—these maidens did not
so.
Therefore my curse is stronger than thy
"throne,"
Thy "suppliance," if by right of laws
eterne
Primeval Justice sits enthroned with
Zeus.
Begone, abhorred, disowned, no son of
mine,
Thou vilest of the vile! and take with
thee
This curse I leave thee as my last
bequest:—
Never to win by arms thy native land,
No, nor return to Argos in the Vale,
But by a kinsman's hand to die and slay
Him who expelled thee. So I pray and
call
On the ancestral gloom of Tartarus
To snatch thee hence, on these dread
goddesses
I call, and Ares who incensed you both
To mortal enmity. Go now proclaim
What thou hast heard to the Cadmeians
all,
Thy staunch confederates—this the
heritage
that Oedipus divideth to his sons.
CHORUS
Thy errand, Polyneices, liked me not
From the beginning; now go back with
speed.
POLYNEICES
Woe worth my journey and my baffled
hopes!

Woe worth my comrades! What a desperate end
To that glad march from Argos! Woe is me!
I dare not whisper it to my allies
Or turn them back, but mute must meet my doom.
My sisters, ye his daughters, ye have heard
The prayers of our stern father, if his curse
Should come to pass and ye some day return
To Thebes, O then disown me not, I pray,
But grant me burial and due funeral rites.
So shall the praise your filial care now wins
Be doubled for the service wrought for me.

ANTIGONE
One boon, O Polyneices, let me crave.

POLYNEICES
What would'st thou, sweet Antigone? Say on.

ANTIGONE
Turn back thy host to Argos with all speed,
And ruin not thyself and Thebes as well.

POLYNEICES
That cannot be. How could I lead again
An army that had seen their leader quail?

ANTIGONE
But, brother, why shouldst thou be wroth again?
What profit from thy country's ruin comes?

POLYNEICES
'Tis shame to live in exile, and shall I
The elder bear a younger brother's flouts?

ANTIGONE
Wilt thou then bring to pass his prophecies

Who threatens mutual slaughter to you both?

POLYNEICES
Aye, so he wishes:—but I must not yield.

ANTIGONE
O woe is me! but say, will any dare,
Hearing his prophecy, to follow thee?

POLYNEICES
I shall not tell it; a good general
Reports successes and conceals mishaps.

ANTIGONE
Misguided youth, thy purpose then stands fast!

POLYNEICES
'Tis so, and stay me not. The road I choose,
Dogged by my sire and his avenging spirit,
Leads me to ruin; but for you may Zeus
Make your path bright if ye fulfill my hest
When dead; in life ye cannot serve me more.
Now let me go, farewell, a long farewell!
Ye ne'er shall see my living face again.

ANTIGONE
Ah me!

POLYNEICES
     Bewail me not.

ANTIGONE
          Who would not mourn
Thee, brother, hurrying to an open pit!

POLYNEICES
If I must die, I must.

ANTIGONE
          Nay, hear me plead.

POLYNEICES
It may not be; forbear.

ANTIGONE
          Then woe is me,
If I must lose thee.

POLYNEICES
          Nay, that rests with fate,
Whether I live or die; but for you both
I pray to heaven ye may escape all ill;

For ye are blameless in the eyes of all.
[Exit POLYNEICES]
CHORUS
(Str. 1)
  Ills on ills! no pause or rest!
  Come they from our sightless guest?
  Or haply now we see fulfilled
  What fate long time hath willed?
  For ne'er have I proved vain
  Aught that the heavenly powers
ordain.
  Time with never sleeping eye
  Watches what is writ on high,
  Overthrowing now the great,
  Raising now from low estate.
Hark! How the thunder rumbles! Zeus
defend us!
OEDIPUS
Children, my children! will no messenger
Go summon hither Theseus my best
friend?
ANTIGONE
And wherefore, father, dost thou
summon him?
OEDIPUS
This winged thunder of the god must
bear me
Anon to Hades. Send and tarry not.
CHORUS
(Ant. 1)
Hark! with louder, nearer roar
The bolt of Zeus descends once more.
My spirit quails and cowers: my hair
Bristles for fear. Again that flare!
What doth the lightning-flash portend?
Ever it points to issues grave.
Dread powers of air! Save, Zeus, O save!
OEDIPUS
Daughters, upon me the predestined end
Has come; no turning from it any more.
ANTIGONE
How knowest thou? What sign
convinces thee?
OEDIPUS

I know full well. Let some one with all
speed
Go summon hither the Athenian prince.
CHORUS
(Str. 2)
Ha! once more the deafening sound
Peals yet louder all around
If thou darkenest our land,
Lightly, lightly lay thy hand;
Grace, not anger, let me win,
If upon a man of sin
I have looked with pitying eye,
Zeus, our king, to thee I cry!
OEDIPUS
Is the prince coming? Will he when he
comes
Find me yet living and my senses clear!
ANTIGONE
What solemn charge would'st thou
impress on him?
OEDIPUS
For all his benefits I would perform
The promise made when I received them
first.
CHORUS
(Ant. 2)
      Hither haste, my son, arise,
      Altar leave and sacrifice,
      If haply to Poseidon now
      In the far glade thou pay'st thy vow.
      For our guest to thee would bring
      And thy folk and offering,
      Thy due guerdon. Haste, O King!
[Enter THESEUS]
THESEUS
Wherefore again this general din? at
once
My people call me and the stranger calls.
Is it a thunderbolt of Zeus or sleet
Of arrowy hail? a storm so fierce as this
Would warrant all surmises of
mischance.
OEDIPUS
Thou com'st much wished for, Prince,
and sure some god

68

Hath bid good luck attend thee on thy
way.
THESEUS
What, son of Laius, hath chanced of new?
OEDIPUS
My life hath turned the scale. I would do
all
I promised thee and thine before I die.
THESEUS
What sign assures thee that thine end is
near?
OEDIPUS
The gods themselves are heralds of my
fate;
Of their appointed warnings nothing
fails.
THESEUS
How sayest thou they signify their will?
OEDIPUS
This thunder, peal on peal, this lightning
hurled
Flash upon flash, from the unconquered
hand.
THESEUS
I must believe thee, having found thee
oft
A prophet true; then speak what must be
done.
OEDIPUS
O son of Aegeus, for this state will I
Unfold a treasure age cannot corrupt.
Myself anon without a guiding hand
Will take thee to the spot where I must
end.
This secret ne'er reveal to mortal man,
Neither the spot nor whereabouts it lies,
So shall it ever serve thee for defense
Better than native shields and near
allies.
But those dread mysteries speech may
not profane
Thyself shalt gather coming there alone;
Since not to any of thy subjects, nor
To my own children, though I love them
dearly,

Can I reveal what thou must guard alone,
And whisper to thy chosen heir alone,
So to be handed down from heir to heir.
Thus shalt thou hold this land inviolate
From the dread Dragon's brood. 7 The
justest State
By countless wanton neighbors may be
wronged,
For the gods, though they tarry, mark for
doom
The godless sinner in his mad career.
Far from thee, son of Aegeus, be such
fate!
But to the spot—the god within me
goads—
Let us set forth no longer hesitate.
Follow me, daughters, this way. Strange
that I
Whom you have led so long should lead
you now.
Oh, touch me not, but let me all alone
Find out the sepulcher that destiny
Appoints me in this land. Hither, this
way,
For this way Hermes leads, the spirit
guide,
And Persephassa, empress of the dead.
O light, no light to me, but mine
erewhile,
Now the last time I feel thee palpable,
For I am drawing near the final gloom
Of Hades. Blessing on thee, dearest
friend,
On thee and on thy land and followers!
Live prosperous and in your happy state
Still for your welfare think on me, the
dead.
[Exit THESEUS followed by ANTIGONE
and ISMENE]
CHORUS
(Str.)

> If mortal prayers are heard in hell,
> Hear, Goddess dread, invisible!
> Monarch of the regions drear,
> Aidoneus, hear, O hear!

By a gentle, tearless doom
Speed this stranger to the gloom,
Let him enter without pain
The all-shrouding Stygian plain.
Wrongfully in life oppressed,
Be he now by Justice blessed.
(Ant.)
Queen infernal, and thou fell
Watch-dog of the gates of hell,
Who, as legends tell, dost glare,
Gnarling in thy cavernous lair
At all comers, let him go
Scathless to the fields below.
For thy master orders thus,
The son of earth and Tartarus;
In his den the monster keep,
Giver of eternal sleep.

[Enter MESSENGER]

MESSENGER
Friends, countrymen, my tidings are in sum
That Oedipus is gone, but the event
Was not so brief, nor can the tale be brief.

CHORUS
What, has he gone, the unhappy man?

MESSENGER
                    Know well
That he has passed away from life to death.

CHORUS
How? By a god-sent, painless doom, poor soul?

MESSENGER
Thy question hits the marvel of the tale.
How he moved hence, you saw him and must know;
Without a friend to lead the way, himself
Guiding us all. So having reached the abrupt
Earth-rooted Threshold with its brazen stairs,
He paused at one of the converging paths,
Hard by the rocky basin which records
The pact of Theseus and Peirithous.
Betwixt that rift and the Thorician rock,
The hollow pear-tree and the marble tomb,
Midway he sat and loosed his beggar's weeds;
Then calling to his daughters bade them fetch
Of running water, both to wash withal
And make libation; so they clomb the steep;
And in brief space brought what their father bade,
Then laved and dressed him with observance due.
But when he had his will in everything,
And no desire was left unsatisfied,
It thundered from the netherworld; the maids
Shivered, and crouching at their father's knees
Wept, beat their breast and uttered a long wail.
He, as he heard their sudden bitter cry,
Folded his arms about them both and said,
"My children, ye will lose your sire today,
For all of me has perished, and no more
Have ye to bear your long, long ministry;
A heavy load, I know, and yet one word
Wipes out all score of tribulations—love
And love from me ye had—from no man more;
But now must live without me all your days."
So clinging to each other sobbed and wept
Father and daughters both, but when at last
Their mourning had an end and no wail rose,
A moment there was silence; suddenly
A voice that summoned him; with sudden dread

70

The hair of all stood up and all were
'mazed;
For the call came, now loud, now low,
and oft.
"Oedipus, Oedipus, why tarry we?
Too long, too long thy passing is
delayed."
But when he heard the summons of the
god,
He prayed that Theseus might be
brought, and when
The Prince came nearer: "O my friend,"
he cried,
"Pledge ye my daughters, giving thy right
hand—
And, daughters, give him yours—and
promise me
Thou never wilt forsake them, but do all
That time and friendship prompt in their
behoof."
And he of his nobility repressed
His tears and swore to be their constant
friend.
This promise given, Oedipus put forth
Blind hands and laid them on his
children, saying,
"O children, prove your true nobility
And hence depart nor seek to witness
sights
Unlawful or to hear unlawful words.
Nay, go with speed; let none but Theseus
stay,
Our ruler, to behold what next shall
hap."
So we all heard him speak, and weeping
sore
We companied the maidens on their
way.
After brief space we looked again, and lo
The man was gone, evanished from our
eyes;
Only the king we saw with upraised
hand
Shading his eyes as from some awful
sight,

That no man might endure to look upon.
A moment later, and we saw him bend
In prayer to Earth and prayer to Heaven
at once.
But by what doom the stranger met his
end
No man save Theseus knoweth. For
there fell
No fiery bold that reft him in that hour,
Nor whirlwind from the sea, but he was
taken.
It was a messenger from heaven, or else
Some gentle, painless cleaving of earth's
base;
For without wailing or disease or pain
He passed away—and end most
marvelous.
And if to some my tale seems foolishness
I am content that such could count me
fool.

CHORUS
Where are the maids and their attendant
friends?

MESSENGER
They cannot be far off; the approaching
sound
Of lamentation tells they come this way.

[Enter ANTIGONE and ISMENE]

ANTIGONE
(Str. 1)
Woe, woe! on this sad day
    We sisters of one blasted stock
    must bow beneath the shock,
Must weep and weep the curse that lay
    On him our sire, for whom
In life, a life-long world of care
    'Twas ours to bear,
    In death must face the gloom
    That wraps his tomb.
What tongue can tell
That sight ineffable?

CHORUS
What mean ye, maidens?

ANTIGONE
                    All is but surmise.

71

CHORUS
Is he then gone?
ANTIGONE
            Gone as ye most might wish.
Not in battle or sea storm,
But reft from sight,
By hands invisible borne
To viewless fields of night.
Ah me! on us too night has come,
The night of mourning. Wither roam
O'er land or sea in our distress
Eating the bread of bitterness?
ISMENE
I know not. O that Death
Might nip my breath,
And let me share my aged father's fate.
I cannot live a life thus desolate.
CHORUS
Best of daughters, worthy pair,
What heaven brings ye needs must bear,
Fret no more 'gainst Heaven's will;
Fate hath dealt with you not ill.
ANTIGONE
(Ant. 1)
Love can turn past pain to bliss,
    What seemed bitter now is sweet.
Ah me! that happy toil is sweet.
    The guidance of those dear blind feet.
Dear father, wrapt for aye in nether
gloom,
    E'en in the tomb
Never shalt thou lack of love repine,
    Her love and mine.
CHORUS
His fate—
ANTIGONE
        Is even as he planned.
CHORUS
How so?
ANTIGONE
He died, so willed he, in a foreign land.
Lapped in kind earth he sleeps his long
last sleep,
    And o'er his grave friends weep.

How great our lost these streaming eyes
can tell,
    This sorrow naught can quell.
Thou hadst thy wish 'mid strangers thus
to die,
    But I, ah me, not by.
ISMENE
Alas, my sister, what new fate
Befalls us orphans desolate?
CHORUS
His end was blessed; therefore, children,
stay
Your sorrow. Man is born to fate a prey.
ANTIGONE
(Str. 2)
Sister, let us back again.
ISMENE
Why return?
ANTIGONE
        My soul is fain—
ISMENE
Is fain?
ANTIGONE
            To see the earthy bed.
ISMENE
Sayest thou?
ANTIGONE
            Where our sire is laid.
ISMENE
Nay, thou can'st not, dost not see—
ANTIGONE
Sister, wherefore wroth with me?
ISMENE
Know'st not—beside—
ANTIGONE
            More must I hear?
ISMENE
Tombless he died, none near.
ANTIGONE
Lead me thither; slay me there.
ISMENE
How shall I unhappy fare,
Friendless, helpless, how drag on
A life of misery alone?
CHORUS

72

(Ant. 2)
Fear not, maids—
ANTIGONE
      Ah, whither flee?
CHORUS
Refuge hath been found.
ANTIGONE
      For me?
CHORUS
Where thou shalt be safe from harm.
ANTIGONE
I know it.
CHORUS
   Why then this alarm?
ANTIGONE
How again to get us home
I know not.
CHORUS
   Why then this roam?
ANTIGONE
Troubles whelm us—
CHORUS
    As of yore.
ANTIGONE
Worse than what was worse before.
CHORUS
Sure ye are driven on the breakers'
surge.
ANTIGONE
Alas! we are.
CHORUS
   Alas! 'tis so.
ANTIGONE
Ah whither turn, O Zeus? No ray
Of hope to cheer the way
Whereon the fates our desperate voyage
urge.
[Enter THESEUS]
THESEUS
Dry your tears; when grace is shed

On the quick and on the dead
By dark Powers beneficent,
Over-grief they would resent.
ANTIGONE
Aegeus' child, to thee we pray.
THESEUS
What the boon, my children, say.
ANTIGONE
With our own eyes we fain would see
Our father's tomb.
THESEUS
    That may not be.
ANTIGONE
What say'st thou, King?
THESEUS
     My children, he
Charged me straitly that no moral
Should approach the sacred portal,
Or greet with funeral litanies
The hidden tomb wherein he lies;
Saying, "If thou keep'st my hest
Thou shalt hold thy realm at rest."
The God of Oaths this promise heard,
And to Zeus I pledged my word.
ANTIGONE
Well, if he would have it so,
We must yield. Then let us go
Back to Thebes, if yet we may
Heal this mortal feud and stay
The self-wrought doom
That drives our brothers to their tomb.
THESEUS
Go in peace; nor will I spare
Ought of toil and zealous care,
But on all your needs attend,
Gladdening in his grave my friend.
CHORUS
Wail no more, let sorrow rest,
All is ordered for the best.

Notes

4. [*The Greek text for the passages marked here and later in the text have been lost.*]

5. [To avoid the blessing, still a secret, he resorts to a commonplace; literally, "For what generous man is not (in befriending others) a friend to himself?"]

6. [Creon desires to bury Oedipus on the confines of Thebes so as to avoid the pollution and yet offer due rites at his tomb. Ismene tells him of the latest oracle and interprets to him its purport, that some day the Theban invaders of Athens will be routed in a battle near the grave of Oedipus.]

7. [The Thebans sprung from the Dragon's teeth sown by Cadmus.]

Antigone

Argument

Antigone, daughter of Oedipus, the late king of Thebes, in defiance of Creon who rules in his stead, resolves to bury her brother Polyneices, slain in his attack on Thebes. She is caught in the act by Creon's watchmen and brought before the king. She justifies her action, asserting that she was bound to obey the eternal laws of right and wrong in spite of any human ordinance. Creon, unrelenting, condemns her to be immured in a rock-hewn chamber. His son Haemon, to whom Antigone is betrothed, pleads in vain for her life and threatens to die with her. Warned by the seer Teiresias Creon repents him and hurries to release Antigone from her rocky prison. But he is too late: he finds lying side by side Antigone who had hanged herself and Haemon who also has perished by his own hand. Returning to the palace he sees within the dead body of his queen who on learning of her son's death has stabbed herself to the heart.

Dramatis Personae

ANTIGONE and ISMENE—daughters of Oedipus and sisters of Polyneices
    and Eteocles.
CREON, King of Thebes.
HAEMON, Son of Creon, betrothed to Antigone.
EURYDICE, wife of Creon.
TEIRESIAS, the prophet.
CHORUS, of Theban elders.
A WATCHMAN
A MESSENGER
A SECOND MESSENGER

Scene: ANTIGONE and ISMENE before the Palace gates.

ANTIGONE
Ismene, sister of my blood and heart,
See'st thou how Zeus would in our lives fulfill
The weird of Oedipus, a world of woes!
For what of pain, affliction, outrage, shame,
Is lacking in our fortunes, thine and mine?
And now this proclamation of today
Made by our Captain-General to the State,
What can its purport be? Didst hear and heed,
Or art thou deaf when friends are banned as foes?
ISMENE
To me, Antigone, no word of friends
Has come, or glad or grievous, since we twain
Were reft of our two brethren in one day
By double fratricide; and since i' the night
Our Argive leaguers fled, no later news
Has reached me, to inspirit or deject.
ANTIGONE
I know 'twas so, and therefore summoned thee
Beyond the gates to breathe it in thine ear.
ISMENE
What is it? Some dark secret stirs thy breast.
ANTIGONE
What but the thought of our two brothers dead,
The one by Creon graced with funeral rites,
The other disappointed? Eteocles
He hath consigned to earth (as fame reports)

With obsequies that use and wont ordain,
So gracing him among the dead below.
But Polyneices, a dishonored corse,
(So by report the royal edict runs)
No man may bury him or make lament—
Must leave him tombless and unwept, a feast
For kites to scent afar and swoop upon.
Such is the edict (if report speak true)
Of Creon, our most noble Creon, aimed
At thee and me, aye me too; and anon
He will be here to promulgate, for such
As have not heard, his mandate; 'tis in sooth
No passing humor, for the edict says
Whoe'er transgresses shall be stoned to death.
So stands it with us; now 'tis thine to show
If thou art worthy of thy blood or base.
ISMENE
But how, my rash, fond sister, in such case
Can I do anything to make or mar?
ANTIGONE
Say, wilt thou aid me and abet? Decide.
ISMENE
In what bold venture? What is in thy thought?
ANTIGONE
Lend me a hand to bear the corpse away.
ISMENE
What, bury him despite the interdict?
ANTIGONE
My brother, and, though thou deny him, thine
No man shall say that I betrayed a brother.
ISMENE
Wilt thou persist, though Creon has forbid?
ANTIGONE
What right has he to keep me from my own?

ISMENE
Bethink thee, sister, of our father's fate,
Abhorred, dishonored, self-convinced of sin,
Blinded, himself his executioner.
Think of his mother-wife (ill sorted names)
Done by a noose herself had twined to death
And last, our hapless brethren in one day,
Both in a mutual destiny involved,
Self-slaughtered, both the slayer and the slain.
Bethink thee, sister, we are left alone;
Shall we not perish wretchedest of all,
If in defiance of the law we cross
A monarch's will?—weak women, think of that,
Not framed by nature to contend with men.
Remember this too that the stronger rules;
We must obey his orders, these or worse.
Therefore I plead compulsion and entreat
The dead to pardon. I perforce obey
The powers that be. 'Tis foolishness, I ween,
To overstep in aught the golden mean.
ANTIGONE
I urge no more; nay, wert thou willing still,
I would not welcome such a fellowship.
Go thine own way; myself will bury him.
How sweet to die in such employ, to rest,—
Sister and brother linked in love's embrace—
A sinless sinner, banned awhile on earth,
But by the dead commended; and with them
I shall abide for ever. As for thee,

Scorn, if thou wilt, the eternal laws of Heaven.
ISMENE
I scorn them not, but to defy the State
Or break her ordinance I have no skill.
ANTIGONE
A specious pretext. I will go alone
To lap my dearest brother in the grave.
ISMENE
My poor, fond sister, how I fear for thee!
ANTIGONE
O waste no fears on me; look to thyself.
ISMENE
At least let no man know of thine intent,
But keep it close and secret, as will I.
ANTIGONE
O tell it, sister; I shall hate thee more
If thou proclaim it not to all the town.
ISMENE
Thou hast a fiery soul for numbing work.
ANTIGONE
I pleasure those whom I would liefest please.
ISMENE
If thou succeed; but thou art doomed to fail.
ANTIGONE
When strength shall fail me, yes, but not before.
ISMENE
But, if the venture's hopeless, why essay?
ANTIGONE
Sister, forbear, or I shall hate thee soon,
And the dead man will hate thee too, with cause.
Say I am mad and give my madness rein
To wreck itself; the worst that can befall
Is but to die an honorable death.
ISMENE
Have thine own way then; 'tis a mad endeavor,
Yet to thy lovers thou art dear as ever.
[Exeunt]
CHORUS

(Str. 1)
Sunbeam, of all that ever dawn upon
    Our seven-gated Thebes the
brightest ray,
      O eye of golden day,
How fair thy light o'er Dirce's fountain
shone,
Speeding upon their headlong
homeward course,
Far quicker than they came, the Argive
force;
      Putting to flight
The argent shields, the host with
scutcheons white.
Against our land the proud invader came
To vindicate fell Polyneices' claim.
    Like to an eagle swooping low,
    On pinions white as new fall'n
snow.
With clanging scream, a horsetail plume
his crest,
The aspiring lord of Argos onward
pressed.
(Ant. 1)
Hovering around our city walls he waits,
His spearmen raven at our seven gates.
But ere a torch our crown of towers
could burn,
Ere they had tasted of our blood, they
turn
Forced by the Dragon; in their rear
The din of Ares panic-struck they hear.
For Zeus who hates the braggart's boast
Beheld that gold-bespangled host;
As at the goal the paean they upraise,
He struck them with his forked lightning
blaze.
(Str. 2)
To earthy from earth rebounding, down
he crashed;
    The fire-brand from his impious hand
was dashed,
As like a Bacchic reveler on he came,
Outbreathing hate and flame,
And tottered. Elsewhere in the field,

Here, there, great Area like a war-horse
wheeled;
      Beneath his car down thrust
      Our foemen bit the dust.
Seven captains at our seven gates
Thundered; for each a champion waits,
Each left behind his armor bright,
Trophy for Zeus who turns the fight;
Save two alone, that ill-starred pair
One mother to one father bare,
Who lance in rest, one 'gainst the other
Drave, and both perished, brother slain
by brother.
(Ant. 2)
Now Victory to Thebes returns again
And smiles upon her chariot-circled
plain.
      Now let feast and festal should
      Memories of war blot out.
      Let us to the temples throng,
      Dance and sing the live night long.
      God of Thebes, lead thou the round.
      Bacchus, shaker of the ground!
      Let us end our revels here;
      Lo! Creon our new lord draws near,
      Crowned by this strange chance,
our king.
      What, I marvel, pondering?
      Why this summons? Wherefore
call
      Us, his elders, one and all,
      Bidding us with him debate,
      On some grave concern of State?
[Enter CREON]
CREON
Elders, the gods have righted one again
Our storm-tossed ship of state, now safe
in port.
But you by special summons I convened
As my most trusted councilors; first,
because
I knew you loyal to Laius of old;
Again, when Oedipus restored our State,
Both while he ruled and when his rule
was o'er,

Ye still were constant to the royal line.
Now that his two sons perished in one day,
Brother by brother murderously slain,
By right of kinship to the Princes dead,
I claim and hold the throne and sovereignty.
Yet 'tis no easy matter to discern
The temper of a man, his mind and will,
Till he be proved by exercise of power;
And in my case, if one who reigns supreme
Swerve from the highest policy, tongue-tied
By fear of consequence, that man I hold,
And ever held, the basest of the base.
And I contemn the man who sets his friend
Before his country. For myself, I call
To witness Zeus, whose eyes are everywhere,
If I perceive some mischievous design
To sap the State, I will not hold my tongue;
Nor would I reckon as my private friend
A public foe, well knowing that the State
Is the good ship that holds our fortunes all:
Farewell to friendship, if she suffers wreck.
Such is the policy by which I seek
To serve the Commons and conformably
I have proclaimed an edict as concerns
The sons of Oedipus; Eteocles
Who in his country's battle fought and fell,
The foremost champion—duly bury him
With all observances and ceremonies
That are the guerdon of the heroic dead.
But for the miscreant exile who returned
Minded in flames and ashes to blot out
His father's city and his father's gods,
And glut his vengeance with his kinsmen's blood,
Or drag them captive at his chariot wheels—
For Polyneices 'tis ordained that none
Shall give him burial or make mourn for him,
But leave his corpse unburied, to be meat
For dogs and carrion crows, a ghastly sight.
So am I purposed; never by my will
Shall miscreants take precedence of true men,
But all good patriots, alive or dead,
Shall be by me preferred and honored.
CHORUS
Son of Menoeceus, thus thou will'st to deal
With him who loathed and him who loved our State.
Thy word is law; thou canst dispose of us
The living, as thou will'st, as of the dead.
CREON
See then ye execute what I ordain.
CHORUS
On younger shoulders lay this grievous charge.
CREON
Fear not, I've posted guards to watch the corpse.
CHORUS
What further duty would'st thou lay on us?
CREON
Not to connive at disobedience.
CHORUS
No man is mad enough to court his death.
CREON
The penalty is death: yet hope of gain
Hath lured men to their ruin oftentimes.
[Enter GUARD]
GUARD
My lord, I will not make pretense to pant
And puff as some light-footed messenger.

In sooth my soul beneath its pack of
thought
Made many a halt and turned and turned
again;
For conscience plied her spur and curb
by turns.
"Why hurry headlong to thy fate, poor
fool?"
She whispered. Then again, "If Creon
learn
This from another, thou wilt rue it
worse."
Thus leisurely I hastened on my road;
Much thought extends a furlong to a
league.
But in the end the forward voice
prevailed,
To face thee. I will speak though I say
nothing.
For plucking courage from despair
methought,
'Let the worst hap, thou canst but meet
thy fate.'
CREON
What is thy news? Why this
despondency?
GUARD
Let me premise a word about myself?
I neither did the deed nor saw it done,
Nor were it just that I should come to
harm.
CREON
Thou art good at parry, and canst fence
about
Some matter of grave import, as is plain.
GUARD
The bearer of dread tidings needs must
quake.
CREON
Then, sirrah, shoot thy bolt and get thee
gone.
GUARD
Well, it must out; the corpse is buried;
someone

E'en now besprinkled it with thirsty
dust,
Performed the proper ritual—and was
gone.
CREON
What say'st thou? Who hath dared to do
this thing?
GUARD
I cannot tell, for there was ne'er a trace
Of pick or mattock—hard unbroken
ground,
Without a scratch or rut of chariot
wheels,
No sign that human hands had been at
work.
When the first sentry of the morning
watch
Gave the alarm, we all were terror-
stricken.
The corpse had vanished, not interred in
earth,
But strewn with dust, as if by one who
sought
To avert the curse that haunts the
unburied dead:
Of hound or ravening jackal, not a sign.
Thereat arose an angry war of words;
Guard railed at guard and blows were
like to end it,
For none was there to part us, each in
turn
Suspected, but the guilt brought home to
none,
From lack of evidence. We challenged
each
The ordeal, or to handle red-hot iron,
Or pass through fire, affirming on our
oath
Our innocence—we neither did the deed
Ourselves, nor know who did or
compassed it.
Our quest was at a standstill, when one
spake
And bowed us all to earth like quivering
reeds,

For there was no gainsaying him nor way
To escape perdition: Yeareboundtotell
TheKing,yecannothideit; so he spake.
And he convinced us all; so lots were cast,
And I, unlucky scapegoat, drew the prize.
So here I am unwilling and withal
Unwelcome; no man cares to hear ill news.

CHORUS
I had misgivings from the first, my liege,
Of something more than natural at work.

CREON
O cease, you vex me with your babblement;
I am like to think you dote in your old age.
Is it not arrant folly to pretend
That gods would have a thought for this dead man?
Did they forsooth award him special grace,
And as some benefactor bury him,
Who came to fire their hallowed sanctuaries,
To sack their shrines, to desolate their land,
And scout their ordinances? Or perchance
The gods bestow their favors on the bad.
No! no! I have long noted malcontents
Who wagged their heads, and kicked against the yoke,
Misliking these my orders, and my rule.
'Tis they, I warrant, who suborned my guards
By bribes. Of evils current upon earth
The worst is money. Money 'tis that sacks
Cities, and drives men forth from hearth and home;
Warps and seduces native innocence,
And breeds a habit of dishonesty.

But they who sold themselves shall find their greed
Out-shot the mark, and rue it soon or late.
Yea, as I still revere the dread of Zeus,
By Zeus I swear, except ye find and bring
Before my presence here the very man
Who carried out this lawless burial,
Death for your punishment shall not suffice.
Hanged on a cross, alive ye first shall make
Confession of this outrage. This will teach you
What practices are like to serve your turn.
There are some villainies that bring no gain.
For by dishonesty the few may thrive,
The many come to ruin and disgrace.

GUARD
May I not speak, or must I turn and go
Without a word?—

CREON
        Begone! canst thou not see
That e'en this question irks me?

GUARD
        Where, my lord?
Is it thy ears that suffer, or thy heart?

CREON
Why seek to probe and find the seat of pain?

GUARD
I gall thine ears—this miscreant thy mind.

CREON
What an inveterate babbler! get thee gone!

GUARD
Babbler perchance, but innocent of the crime.

CREON
Twice guilty, having sold thy soul for gain.

GUARD

Alas! how sad when reasoners reason wrong.

CREON

Go, quibble with thy reason. If thou fail'st
To find these malefactors, thou shalt own
The wages of ill-gotten gains is death.

[Exit CREON]

GUARD

I pray he may be found. But caught or not
(And fortune must determine that) thou never
Shalt see me here returning; that is sure.
For past all hope or thought I have escaped,
And for my safety owe the gods much thanks.

CHORUS

(Str. 1)

Many wonders there be, but naught more wondrous than man;
Over the surging sea, with a whitening south wind wan,
Through the foam of the firth, man makes his perilous way;
And the eldest of deities Earth that knows not toil nor decay
Ever he furrows and scores, as his team, year in year out,
With breed of the yoked horse, the ploughshare turneth about.

(Ant. 1)

The light-witted birds of the air, the beasts of the weald and the wood
He traps with his woven snare, and the brood of the briny flood.
Master of cunning he: the savage bull, and the hart
Who roams the mountain free, are tamed by his infinite art;
And the shaggy rough-maned steed is broken to bear the bit.

(Str. 2)

Speech and the wind-swift speed of counsel and civic wit,
He hath learnt for himself all these; and the arrowy rain to fly
And the nipping airs that freeze, 'neath the open winter sky.
He hath provision for all: fell plague he hath learnt to endure;
Safe whate'er may befall: yet for death he hath found no cure.

(Ant. 2)

Passing the wildest flight thought are the cunning and skill,
That guide man now to the light, but now to counsels of ill.
If he honors the laws of the land, and reveres the Gods of the State
Proudly his city shall stand; but a cityless outcast I rate
Whoso bold in his pride from the path of right doth depart;
Ne'er may I sit by his side, or share the thoughts of his heart.

What strange vision meets my eyes,
Fills me with a wild surprise?
Sure I know her, sure 'tis she,
The maid Antigone.
Hapless child of hapless sire,
Didst thou recklessly conspire,
Madly brave the King's decree?
Therefore are they haling thee?

[Enter GUARD bringing ANTIGONE]

GUARD

Here is the culprit taken in the act
Of giving burial. But where's the King?

CHORUS

There from the palace he returns in time.

[Enter CREON]

CREON

Why is my presence timely? What has chanced?

GUARD

No man, my lord, should make a vow, for if
He ever swears he will not do a thing,

His afterthoughts belie his first resolve.
When from the hail-storm of thy threats I fled
I sware thou wouldst not see me here again;
But the wild rapture of a glad surprise
Intoxicates, and so I'm here forsworn.
And here's my prisoner, caught in the very act,
Decking the grave. No lottery this time;
This prize is mine by right of treasure-trove.
So take her, judge her, rack her, if thou wilt.
She's thine, my liege; but I may rightly claim
Hence to depart well quit of all these ills.

CREON
Say, how didst thou arrest the maid, and where?

GUARD
Burying the man. There's nothing more to tell.

CREON
Hast thou thy wits? Or know'st thou what thou say'st?

GUARD
I saw this woman burying the corpse
Against thy orders. Is that clear and plain?

CREON
But how was she surprised and caught in the act?

GUARD
It happened thus. No sooner had we come,
Driven from thy presence by those awful threats,
Than straight we swept away all trace of dust,
And bared the clammy body. Then we sat
High on the ridge to windward of the stench,
While each man kept he fellow alert and rated
Roundly the sluggard if he chanced to nap.
So all night long we watched, until the sun
Stood high in heaven, and his blazing beams
Smote us. A sudden whirlwind then upraised
A cloud of dust that blotted out the sky,
And swept the plain, and stripped the woodlands bare,
And shook the firmament. We closed our eyes
And waited till the heaven-sent plague should pass.
At last it ceased, and lo! there stood this maid.
A piercing cry she uttered, sad and shrill,
As when the mother bird beholds her nest
Robbed of its nestlings; even so the maid
Wailed as she saw the body stripped and bare,
And cursed the ruffians who had done this deed.
Anon she gathered handfuls of dry dust,
Then, holding high a well-wrought brazen urn,
Thrice on the dead she poured a lustral stream.
We at the sight swooped down on her and seized
Our quarry. Undismayed she stood, and when
We taxed her with the former crime and this,
She disowned nothing. I was glad—and grieved;
For 'tis most sweet to 'scape oneself scot-free,
And yet to bring disaster to a friend
Is grievous. Take it all in all, I deem
A man's first duty is to serve himself.

CREON
Speak, girl, with head bent low and downcast eyes,
Does thou plead guilty or deny the deed?
ANTIGONE
Guilty. I did it, I deny it not.
CREON (to GUARD)
Sirrah, begone whither thou wilt, and thank
Thy luck that thou hast 'scaped a heavy charge.
(To ANTIGONE)
Now answer this plain question, yes or no,
Wast thou acquainted with the interdict?
ANTIGONE
I knew, all knew; how should I fail to know?
CREON
And yet wert bold enough to break the law?
ANTIGONE
Yea, for these laws were not ordained of Zeus,
And she who sits enthroned with gods below,
Justice, enacted not these human laws.
Nor did I deem that thou, a mortal man,
Could'st by a breath annul and override
The immutable unwritten laws of Heaven.
They were not born today nor yesterday;
They die not; and none knoweth whence they sprang.
I was not like, who feared no mortal's frown,
To disobey these laws and so provoke
The wrath of Heaven. I knew that I must die,
E'en hadst thou not proclaimed it; and if death
Is thereby hastened, I shall count it gain.
For death is gain to him whose life, like mine,
Is full of misery. Thus my lot appears

Not sad, but blissful; for had I endured
To leave my mother's son unburied there,
I should have grieved with reason, but not now.
And if in this thou judgest me a fool,
Methinks the judge of folly's not acquit.
CHORUS
A stubborn daughter of a stubborn sire,
This ill-starred maiden kicks against the pricks.
CREON
Well, let her know the stubbornest of wills
Are soonest bended, as the hardest iron,
O'er-heated in the fire to brittleness,
Flies soonest into fragments, shivered through.
A snaffle curbs the fieriest steed, and he
Who in subjection lives must needs be meek.
But this proud girl, in insolence well-schooled,
First overstepped the established law, and then—
A second and worse act of insolence—
She boasts and glories in her wickedness.
Now if she thus can flout authority
Unpunished, I am woman, she the man.
But though she be my sister's child or nearer
Of kin than all who worship at my hearth,
Nor she nor yet her sister shall escape
The utmost penalty, for both I hold,
As arch-conspirators, of equal guilt.
Bring forth the older; even now I saw her
Within the palace, frenzied and distraught.
The workings of the mind discover oft
Dark deeds in darkness schemed, before the act.

More hateful still the miscreant who seeks
When caught, to make a virtue of a crime.
ANTIGONE
Would'st thou do more than slay thy prisoner?
CREON
Not I, thy life is mine, and that's enough.
ANTIGONE
Why dally then? To me no word of thine
Is pleasant: God forbid it e'er should please;
Nor am I more acceptable to thee.
And yet how otherwise had I achieved
A name so glorious as by burying
A brother? so my townsmen all would say,
Where they not gagged by terror, Manifold
A king's prerogatives, and not the least
That all his acts and all his words are law.
CREON
Of all these Thebans none so deems but thou.
ANTIGONE
These think as I, but bate their breath to thee.
CREON
Hast thou no shame to differ from all these?
ANTIGONE
To reverence kith and kin can bring no shame.
CREON
Was his dead foeman not thy kinsman too?
ANTIGONE
One mother bare them and the self-same sire.
CREON
Why cast a slur on one by honoring one?
ANTIGONE

The dead man will not bear thee out in this.
CREON
Surely, if good and evil fare alive.
ANTIGONE
The slain man was no villain but a brother.
CREON
The patriot perished by the outlaw's brand.
ANTIGONE
Nathless the realms below these rites require.
CREON
Not that the base should fare as do the brave.
ANTIGONE
Who knows if this world's crimes are virtues there?
CREON
Not even death can make a foe a friend.
ANTIGONE
My nature is for mutual love, not hate.
CREON
Die then, and love the dead if thou must;
No woman shall be the master while I live.
[Enter ISMENE]
CHORUS
    Lo from out the palace gate,
    Weeping o'er her sister's fate,
    Comes Ismene; see her brow,
    Once serene, beclouded now,
    See her beauteous face o'erspread
    With a flush of angry red.
CREON
Woman, who like a viper unperceived
Didst harbor in my house and drain my blood,
Two plagues I nurtured blindly, so it proved,
To sap my throne. Say, didst thou too abet
This crime, or dost abjure all privity?
ISMENE

I did the deed, if she will have it so,
And with my sister claim to share the guilt.
ANTIGONE
That were unjust. Thou would'st not act with me
At first, and I refused thy partnership.
ISMENE
But now thy bark is stranded, I am bold
To claim my share as partner in the loss.
ANTIGONE
Who did the deed the under-world knows well:
A friend in word is never friend of mine.
ISMENE
O sister, scorn me not, let me but share
Thy work of piety, and with thee die.
ANTIGONE
Claim not a work in which thou hadst no hand;
One death sufficeth. Wherefore should'st thou die?
ISMENE
What would life profit me bereft of thee?
ANTIGONE
Ask Creon, he's thy kinsman and best friend.
ISMENE
Why taunt me? Find'st thou pleasure in these gibes?
ANTIGONE
'Tis a sad mockery, if indeed I mock.
ISMENE
O say if I can help thee even now.
ANTIGONE
No, save thyself; I grudge not thy escape.
ISMENE
Is e'en this boon denied, to share thy lot?
ANTIGONE
Yea, for thou chosed'st life, and I to die.
ISMENE
Thou canst not say that I did not protest.
ANTIGONE
Well, some approved thy wisdom, others mine.

ISMENE
But now we stand convicted, both alike.
ANTIGONE
Fear not; thou livest, I died long ago
Then when I gave my life to save the dead.
CREON
Both maids, methinks, are crazed. One suddenly
Has lost her wits, the other was born mad.
ISMENE
Yea, so it falls, sire, when misfortune comes,
The wisest even lose their mother wit.
CREON
I' faith thy wit forsook thee when thou mad'st
Thy choice with evil-doers to do ill.
ISMENE
What life for me without my sister here?
CREON
Say not thy sister here: thy sister's dead.
ISMENE
What, wilt thou slay thy own son's plighted bride?
CREON
Aye, let him raise him seed from other fields.
ISMENE
No new espousal can be like the old.
CREON
A plague on trulls who court and woo our sons.
ANTIGONE
O Haemon, how thy sire dishonors thee!
CREON
A plague on thee and thy accursed bride!
CHORUS
What, wilt thou rob thine own son of his bride?
CREON
'Tis death that bars this marriage, not his sire.
CHORUS

So her death-warrant, it would seem, is sealed.

CREON

By you, as first by me; off with them, guards,
And keep them close. Henceforward let them learn
To live as women use, not roam at large.
For e'en the bravest spirits run away
When they perceive death pressing on life's heels.

CHORUS

(Str. 1)

Thrice blest are they who never tasted pain!
    If once the curse of Heaven attaint a race,
    The infection lingers on and speeds apace,
Age after age, and each the cup must drain.
So when Etesian blasts from Thrace downpour
    Sweep o'er the blackening main and whirl to land
    From Ocean's cavernous depths his ooze and sand,
Billow on billow thunders on the shore.

(Ant. 1)

On the Labdacidae I see descending
    Woe upon woe; from days of old some god
    Laid on the race a malison, and his rod
Scourges each age with sorrows never ending.
The light that dawned upon its last born son
    Is vanished, and the bloody axe of Fate
    Has felled the goodly tree that blossomed late.
O Oedipus, by reckless pride undone!

(Str. 2)

Thy might, O Zeus, what mortal power can quell?

Not sleep that lays all else beneath its spell,
Nor moons that never tire: untouched by Time,
    Throned in the dazzling light
    That crowns Olympus' height,
Thou reignest King, omnipotent, sublime.
    Past, present, and to be,
    All bow to thy decree,
    All that exceeds the mean by Fate
    Is punished, Love or Hate.

(Ant. 2)

Hope flits about never-wearying wings;
Profit to some, to some light loves she brings,
But no man knoweth how her gifts may turn,
Till 'neath his feet the treacherous ashes burn.
Sure 'twas a sage inspired that spake this word;
    If evil good appear
    To any, Fate is near;
And brief the respite from her flaming sword.
    Hither comes in angry mood
    Haemon, latest of thy brood;
    Is it for his bride he's grieved,
    Or her marriage-bed deceived,
    Doth he make his mourn for thee,
    Maid forlorn, Antigone?

[Enter HAEMON]

CREON

Soon shall we know, better than seer can tell.
Learning may fixed decree anent thy bride,
Thou mean'st not, son, to rave against thy sire?
Know'st not whate'er we do is done in love?

HAEMON

O father, I am thine, and I will take
Thy wisdom as the helm to steer withal.

Therefore no wedlock shall by me be held
More precious than thy loving goverance.

CREON

Well spoken: so right-minded sons should feel,
In all deferring to a father's will.
For 'tis the hope of parents they may rear
A brood of sons submissive, keen to avenge
Their father's wrongs, and count his friends their own.
But who begets unprofitable sons,
He verily breeds trouble for himself,
And for his foes much laughter. Son, be warned
And let no woman fool away thy wits.
Ill fares the husband mated with a shrew,
And her embraces very soon wax cold.
For what can wound so surely to the quick
As a false friend? So spue and cast her off,
Bid her go find a husband with the dead.
For since I caught her openly rebelling,
Of all my subjects the one malcontent,
I will not prove a traitor to the State.
She surely dies. Go, let her, if she will,
Appeal to Zeus the God of Kindred, for
If thus I nurse rebellion in my house,
Shall not I foster mutiny without?
For whoso rules his household worthily,
Will prove in civic matters no less wise.
But he who overbears the laws, or thinks
To overrule his rulers, such as one
I never will allow. Whome'er the State
Appoints must be obeyed in everything,
But small and great, just and unjust alike.
I warrant such a one in either case
Would shine, as King or subject; such a man

Would in the storm of battle stand his ground,
A comrade leal and true; but Anarchy—
What evils are not wrought by Anarchy!
She ruins States, and overthrows the home,
She dissipates and routs the embattled host;
While discipline preserves the ordered ranks.
Therefore we must maintain authority
And yield to title to a woman's will.
Better, if needs be, men should cast us out
Than hear it said, a woman proved his match.

CHORUS

To me, unless old age have dulled wits,
Thy words appear both reasonable and wise.

HAEMON

Father, the gods implant in mortal men
Reason, the choicest gift bestowed by heaven.
'Tis not for me to say thou errest, nor
Would I arraign thy wisdom, if I could;
And yet wise thoughts may come to other men
And, as thy son, it falls to me to mark
The acts, the words, the comments of the crowd.
The commons stand in terror of thy frown,
And dare not utter aught that might offend,
But I can overhear their muttered plaints,
Know how the people mourn this maiden doomed
For noblest deeds to die the worst of deaths.
When her own brother slain in battle lay
Unsepulchered, she suffered not his corse
To lie for carrion birds and dogs to maul:

Should not her name (they cry) be writ
in gold?
Such the low murmurings that reach my
ear.
O father, nothing is by me more prized
Than thy well-being, for what higher
good
Can children covet than their sire's fair
fame,
As fathers too take pride in glorious
sons?
Therefore, my father, cling not to one
mood,
And deemed not thou art right, all others
wrong.
For whoso thinks that wisdom dwells
with him,
That he alone can speak or think aright,
Such oracles are empty breath when
tried.
The wisest man will let himself be
swayed
By others' wisdom and relax in time.
See how the trees beside a stream in
flood
Save, if they yield to force, each spray
unharmed,
But by resisting perish root and branch.
The mariner who keeps his mainsheet
taut,
And will not slacken in the gale, is like
To sail with thwarts reversed, keel
uppermost.
Relent then and repent thee of thy
wrath;
For, if one young in years may claim
some sense,
I'll say 'tis best of all to be endowed
With absolute wisdom; but, if that's
denied,
(And nature takes not readily that ply)
Next wise is he who lists to sage advice.
CHORUS
If he says aught in season, heed him,
King.

(To HAEMON)
Heed thou thy sire too; both have spoken
well.
CREON
What, would you have us at our age be
schooled,
Lessoned in prudence by a beardless
boy?
HAEMON
I plead for justice, father, nothing more.
Weigh me upon my merit, not my years.
CREON
Strange merit this to sanction
lawlessness!
HAEMON
For evil-doers I would urge no plea.
CREON
Is not this maid an arrant law-breaker?
HAEMON
The Theban commons with one voice
say, No.
CREON
What, shall the mob dictate my policy?
HAEMON
'Tis thou, methinks, who speakest like a
boy.
CREON
Am I to rule for others, or myself?
HAEMON
A State for one man is no State at all.
CREON
The State is his who rules it, so 'tis held.
HAEMON
As monarch of a desert thou wouldst
shine.
CREON
This boy, methinks, maintains the
woman's cause.
HAEMON
If thou be'st woman, yes. My thought's
for thee.
CREON
O reprobate, would'st wrangle with thy
sire?
HAEMON

Because I see thee wrongfully perverse.
CREON
And am I wrong, if I maintain my rights?
HAEMON
Talk not of rights; thou spurn'st the due
of Heaven
CREON
O heart corrupt, a woman's minion thou!
HAEMON
Slave to dishonor thou wilt never find
me.
CREON
Thy speech at least was all a plea for her.
HAEMON
And thee and me, and for the gods
below.
CREON
Living the maid shall never be thy bride.
HAEMON
So she shall die, but one will die with
her.
CREON
Hast come to such a pass as threaten
me?
HAEMON
What threat is this, vain counsels to
reprove?
CREON
Vain fool to instruct thy betters; thou
shall rue it.
HAEMON
Wert not my father, I had said thou
err'st.
CREON
Play not the spaniel, thou a woman's
slave.
HAEMON
When thou dost speak, must no man
make reply?
CREON
This passes bounds. By heaven, thou
shalt not rate
And jeer and flout me with impunity.
Off with the hateful thing that she may
die

At once, beside her bridegroom, in his
sight.
HAEMON
Think not that in my sight the maid shall
die,
Or by my side; never shalt thou again
Behold my face hereafter. Go, consort
With friends who like a madman for
their mate.
[Exit HAEMON]
CHORUS
Thy son has gone, my liege, in angry
haste.
Fell is the wrath of youth beneath a
smart.
CREON
Let him go vent his fury like a fiend:
These sisters twain he shall not save
from death.
CHORUS
Surely, thou meanest not to slay them
both?
CREON
I stand corrected; only her who touched
The body.
CHORUS
        And what death is she to die?
CREON
She shall be taken to some desert place
By man untrod, and in a rock-hewn cave,
With food no more than to avoid the
taint
That homicide might bring on all the
State,
Buried alive. There let her call in aid
The King of Death, the one god she
reveres,
Or learn too late a lesson learnt at last:
'Tis labor lost, to reverence the dead.
CHORUS
(Str.)
Love resistless in fight, all yield at a
glance of thine eye,
Love who pillowed all night on a
maiden's cheek dost lie,

Over the upland holds. Shall mortals not yield to thee?
(Ant).
Mad are thy subjects all, and even the wisest heart
Straight to folly will fall, at a touch of thy poisoned dart.
Thou didst kindle the strife, this feud of kinsman with kin,
By the eyes of a winsome wife, and the yearning her heart to win.
For as her consort still, enthroned with Justice above,
Thou bendest man to thy will, O all invincible Love.

> Lo I myself am borne aside,
> From Justice, as I view this bride.
> (O sight an eye in tears to drown)
> Antigone, so young, so fair,
>> Thus hurried down
> Death's bower with the dead to share.

ANTIGONE
(Str. 1)
Friends, countrymen, my last farewell I make;
> My journey's done.
One last fond, lingering, longing look I take
> At the bright sun.
For Death who puts to sleep both young and old
> Hales my young life,
And beckons me to Acheron's dark fold,
> An unwed wife.
No youths have sung the marriage song for me,
> My bridal bed
No maids have strewn with flowers from the lea,
> 'Tis Death I wed.

CHORUS
> But bethink thee, thou art sped,
> Great and glorious, to the dead.

Thou the sword's edge hast not tasted,
> No disease thy frame hath wasted.
> Freely thou alone shalt go
> Living to the dead below.

ANTIGONE
(Ant. 1)
Nay, but the piteous tale I've heard men tell
> Of Tantalus' doomed child,
Chained upon Siphylus' high rocky fell,
> That clung like ivy wild,
Drenched by the pelting rain and whirling snow,
> Left there to pine,
While on her frozen breast the tears aye flow—
> Her fate is mine.

CHORUS
> She was sprung of gods, divine,
> Mortals we of mortal line.
> Like renown with gods to gain
> Recompenses all thy pain.
> Take this solace to thy tomb
> Hers in life and death thy doom.

ANTIGONE
(Str. 2)
Alack, alack! Ye mock me. Is it meet
> Thus to insult me living, to my face?
Cease, by our country's altars I entreat,
> Ye lordly rulers of a lordly race.
O fount of Dirce, wood-embowered plain
> Where Theban chariots to victory speed,
Mark ye the cruel laws that now have wrought my bane,
> The friends who show no pity in my need!
Was ever fate like mine? O monstrous doom,
> Within a rock-built prison sepulchered,
To fade and wither in a living tomb,
> And alien midst the living and the dead.

CHORUS
(Str. 3)
> In thy boldness over-rash
> Madly thou thy foot didst dash
> 'Gainst high Justice' altar stair.
> Thou a father's guild dost bear.

ANTIGONE
(Ant. 2)
At this thou touchest my most poignant pain,
> My ill-starred father's piteous disgrace,
The taint of blood, the hereditary stain,
> That clings to all of Labdacus' famed race.
Woe worth the monstrous marriage-bed where lay
> A mother with the son her womb had borne,
Therein I was conceived, woe worth the day,
> Fruit of incestuous sheets, a maid forlorn,
And now I pass, accursed and unwed,
> To meet them as an alien there below;
And thee, O brother, in marriage ill-bestead,
> 'Twas thy dead hand that dealt me this death-blow.

CHORUS
> Religion has her chains, 'tis true,
> Let rite be paid when rites are due.
> Yet is it ill to disobey
> The powers who hold by might the sway.
> Thou hast withstood authority,
> A self-willed rebel, thou must die.

ANTIGONE
Unwept, unwed, unfriended, hence I go,
> No longer may I see the day's bright eye;
Not one friend left to share my bitter woe,
> And o'er my ashes heave one passing sigh.

CREON
If wail and lamentation aught availed
To stave off death, I trow they'd never end.
Away with her, and having walled her up
In a rock-vaulted tomb, as I ordained,
Leave her alone at liberty to die,
Or, if she choose, to live in solitude,
The tomb her dwelling. We in either case
Are guiltless as concerns this maiden's blood,
Only on earth no lodging shall she find.

ANTIGONE
O grave, O bridal bower, O prison house
Hewn from the rock, my everlasting home,
Whither I go to join the mighty host
Of kinsfolk, Persephassa's guests long dead,
The last of all, of all more miserable,
I pass, my destined span of years cut short.
And yet good hope is mine that I shall find
A welcome from my sire, a welcome too,
From thee, my mother, and my brother dear;
From with these hands, I laved and decked your limbs
In death, and poured libations on your grave.
And last, my Polyneices, unto thee
I paid due rites, and this my recompense!
Yet am I justified in wisdom's eyes.
For even had it been some child of mine,
Or husband mouldering in death's decay,
I had not wrought this deed despite the State.
What is the law I call in aid? 'Tis thus
I argue. Had it been a husband dead
I might have wed another, and have borne

Another child, to take the dead child's place.
But, now my sire and mother both are dead,
No second brother can be born for me.
Thus by the law of conscience I was led
To honor thee, dear brother, and was judged
By Creon guilty of a heinous crime.
And now he drags me like a criminal,
A bride unwed, amerced of marriage-song
And marriage-bed and joys of motherhood,
By friends deserted to a living grave.
What ordinance of heaven have I transgressed?
Hereafter can I look to any god
For succor, call on any man for help?
Alas, my piety is impious deemed.
Well, if such justice is approved of heaven,
I shall be taught by suffering my sin;
But if the sin is theirs, O may they suffer
No worse ills than the wrongs they do to me.

CHORUS
The same ungovernable will
Drives like a gale the maiden still.

CREON
Therefore, my guards who let her stay
Shall smart full sore for their delay.

ANTIGONE
Ah, woe is me! This word I hear
Brings death most near.

CHORUS
I have no comfort. What he saith,
Portends no other thing than death.

ANTIGONE
My fatherland, city of Thebes divine,
Ye gods of Thebes whence sprang my line,
Look, puissant lords of Thebes, on me;
The last of all your royal house ye see.
Martyred by men of sin, undone.

Such meed my piety hath won.
[Exit ANTIGONE]
CHORUS
(Str. 1)
Like to thee that maiden bright,
    Danae, in her brass-bound tower,
Once exchanged the glad sunlight
    For a cell, her bridal bower.
And yet she sprang of royal line,
    My child, like thine,
    And nursed the seed
    By her conceived
Of Zeus descending in a golden shower.
Strange are the ways of Fate, her power
Nor wealth, nor arms withstand, nor tower;
Nor brass-prowed ships, that breast the sea
    From Fate can flee.
(Ant. 1)
Thus Dryas' child, the rash Edonian King,
For words of high disdain
Did Bacchus to a rocky dungeon bring,
To cool the madness of a fevered brain.
    His frenzy passed,
    He learnt at last
'Twas madness gibes against a god to fling.
For once he fain had quenched the Maenad's fire;
And of the tuneful Nine provoked the ire.
(Str. 2)
By the Iron Rocks that guard the double main,
    On Bosporus' lone strand,
Where stretcheth Salmydessus' plain
    In the wild Thracian land,
There on his borders Ares witnessed
    The vengeance by a jealous step-dame ta'en
The gore that trickled from a spindle red,
    The sightless orbits of her step-sons twain.
(Ant. 2)

Wasting away they mourned their
piteous doom,
The blasted issue of their mother's
womb.
But she her lineage could trace
    To great Erechtheus' race;
Daughter of Boreas in her sire's vast
caves
    Reared, where the tempest raves,
Swift as his horses o'er the hills she
sped;
A child of gods; yet she, my child, like
thee,
    By Destiny
That knows not death nor age—she too
was vanquished.

[Enter TEIRESIAS and BOY]

TEIRESIAS

Princes of Thebes, two wayfarers as one,
Having betwixt us eyes for one, we are
here.
The blind man cannot move without a
guide.

CREON

Why tidings, old Teiresias?

TEIRESIAS

           I will tell thee;
And when thou hearest thou must heed
the seer.

CREON

Thus far I ne'er have disobeyed thy rede.

TEIRESIAS

So hast thou steered the ship of State
aright.

CREON

I know it, and I gladly own my debt.

TEIRESIAS

Bethink thee that thou treadest once
again
The razor edge of peril.

CREON

          What is this?
Thy words inspire a dread presentiment.

TEIRESIAS

The divination of my arts shall tell.

Sitting upon my throne of augury,
As is my wont, where every fowl of
heaven
Find harborage, upon mine ears was
borne
A jargon strange of twitterings, hoots,
and screams;
So knew I that each bird at the other tare
With bloody talons, for the whirr of
wings
Could signify naught else. Perturbed in
soul,
I straight essayed the sacrifice by fire
On blazing altars, but the God of Fire
Came not in flame, and from the thigh
bones dripped
And sputtered in the ashes a foul ooze;
Gall-bladders cracked and spurted up:
the fat
Melted and fell and left the thigh bones
bare.
Such are the signs, taught by this lad, I
read—
As I guide others, so the boy guides me—
The frustrate signs of oracles grown
dumb.
O King, thy willful temper ails the State,
For all our shrines and altars are
profaned
By what has filled the maw of dogs and
crows,
The flesh of Oedipus' unburied son.
Therefore the angry gods abominate
Our litanies and our burnt offerings;
Therefore no birds trill out a happy note,
Gorged with the carnival of human gore.
O ponder this, my son. To err is common
To all men, but the man who having
erred
Hugs not his errors, but repents and
seeks
The cure, is not a wastrel nor unwise.
No fool, the saw goes, like the obstinate
fool.

Let death disarm thy vengeance. O forbear
To vex the dead. What glory wilt thou win
By slaying twice the slain? I mean thee well;
Counsel's most welcome if I promise gain.
CREON
Old man, ye all let fly at me your shafts
Like anchors at a target; yea, ye set
Your soothsayer on me. Peddlers are ye all
And I the merchandise ye buy and sell.
Go to, and make your profit where ye will,
Silver of Sardis change for gold of Ind;
Ye will not purchase this man's burial,
Not though the winged ministers of Zeus
Should bear him in their talons to his throne;
Not e'en in awe of prodigy so dire
Would I permit his burial, for I know
No human soilure can assail the gods;
This too I know, Teiresias, dire's the fall
Of craft and cunning when it tries to gloss
Foul treachery with fair words for filthy gain.
TEIRESIAS
Alas! doth any know and lay to heart—
CREON
Is this the prelude to some hackneyed saw?
TEIRESIAS
How far good counsel is the best of goods?
CREON
True, as unwisdom is the worst of ills.
TEIRESIAS
Thou art infected with that ill thyself.
CREON
I will not bandy insults with thee, seer.
TEIRESIAS

And yet thou say'st my prophesies are frauds.
CREON
Prophets are all a money-getting tribe.
TEIRESIAS
And kings are all a lucre-loving race.
CREON
Dost know at whom thou glancest, me thy lord?
TEIRESIAS
Lord of the State and savior, thanks to me.
CREON
Skilled prophet art thou, but to wrong inclined.
TEIRESIAS
Take heed, thou wilt provoke me to reveal
The mystery deep hidden in my breast.
CREON
Say on, but see it be not said for gain.
TEIRESIAS
Such thou, methinks, till now hast judged my words.
CREON
Be sure thou wilt not traffic on my wits.
TEIRESIAS
Know then for sure, the coursers of the sun
Not many times shall run their race, before
Thou shalt have given the fruit of thine own loins
In quittance of thy murder, life for life;
For that thou hast entombed a living soul,
And sent below a denizen of earth,
And wronged the nether gods by leaving here
A corpse unlaved, unwept, unsepulchered.
Herein thou hast no part, nor e'en the gods
In heaven; and thou usurp'st a power not thine.

For this the avenging spirits of Heaven
and Hell
Who dog the steps of sin are on thy trail:
What these have suffered thou shalt
suffer too.
And now, consider whether bought by
gold
I prophesy. For, yet a little while,
And sound of lamentation shall be heard,
Of men and women through thy desolate
halls;
And all thy neighbor States are leagues
to avenge
Their mangled warriors who have found
a grave
I' the maw of wolf or hound, or winged
bird
That flying homewards taints their city's
air.
These are the shafts, that like a bowman
I
Provoked to anger, loosen at thy breast,
Unerring, and their smart thou shalt not
shun.
Boy, lead me home, that he may vent his
spleen
On younger men, and learn to curb his
tongue
With gentler manners than his present
mood.
[Exit TEIRESIAS]
CHORUS
My liege, that man hath gone, foretelling
woe.
And, O believe me, since these grizzled
locks
Were like the raven, never have I known
The prophet's warning to the State to
fail.
CREON
I know it too, and it perplexes me.
To yield is grievous, but the obstinate
soul
That fights with Fate, is smitten
grievously.

CHORUS
Son of Menoeceus, list to good advice.
CHORUS
What should I do. Advise me. I will
heed.
CHORUS
Go, free the maiden from her rocky cell;
And for the unburied outlaw build a
tomb.
CREON
Is that your counsel? You would have
me yield?
CHORUS
Yea, king, this instant. Vengeance of the
gods
Is swift to overtake the impenitent.
CREON
Ah! what a wrench it is to sacrifice
My heart's resolve; but Fate is ill to fight.
CHORUS
Go, trust not others. Do it quick thyself.
CREON
I go hot-foot. Bestir ye one and all,
My henchmen! Get ye axes! Speed away
To yonder eminence! I too will go,
For all my resolution this way sways.
'Twas I that bound, I too will set her free.
Almost I am persuaded it is best
To keep through life the law ordained of
old.
[Exit CREON]
CHORUS
(Str. 1)
Thou by many names adored,
    Child of Zeus the God of thunder,
    Of a Theban bride the wonder,
Fair Italia's guardian lord;
In the deep-embosomed glades
    Of the Eleusinian Queen
Haunt of revelers, men and maids,
    Dionysus, thou art seen.
Where Ismenus rolls his waters,
    Where the Dragon's teeth were
sown,
Where the Bacchanals thy daughters

Round thee roam,
There thy home;
Thebes, O Bacchus, is thine own.
(Ant. 1)
Thee on the two-crested rock
    Lurid-flaming torches see;
Where Corisian maidens flock,
    Thee the springs of Castaly.
By Nysa's bastion ivy-clad,
By shores with clustered vineyards glad,
There to thee the hymn rings out,
And through our streets we Thebans
shout,
    All hall to thee
    Evoe, Evoe!
(Str. 2)
Oh, as thou lov'st this city best of all,
To thee, and to thy Mother levin-
stricken,
In our dire need we call;
Thou see'st with what a plague our
townsfolk sicken.
    Thy ready help we crave,
Whether adown Parnassian heights
descending,
Or o'er the roaring straits thy swift was
wending,
    Save us, O save!
(Ant. 2)
Brightest of all the orbs that breathe
forth light,
    Authentic son of Zeus, immortal king,
Leader of all the voices of the night,
    Come, and thy train of Thyiads with
thee bring,
    Thy maddened rout
Who dance before thee all night long,
and shout,
    Thy handmaids we,
    Evoe, Evoe!
[Enter MESSENGER]
MESSENGER
Attend all ye who dwell beside the halls
Of Cadmus and Amphion. No man's life
As of one tenor would I praise or blame,

For Fortune with a constant ebb and rise
Casts down and raises high and low
alike,
And none can read a mortal's horoscope.
Take Creon; he, methought, if any man,
Was enviable. He had saved this land
Of Cadmus from our enemies and
attained
A monarch's powers and ruled the state
supreme,
While a right noble issue crowned his
bliss.
Now all is gone and wasted, for a life
Without life's joys I count a living death.
You'll tell me he has ample store of
wealth,
The pomp and circumstance of kings;
but if
These give no pleasure, all the rest I
count
The shadow of a shade, nor would I
weigh
His wealth and power 'gainst a dram of
joy.
CHORUS
What fresh woes bring'st thou to the
royal house?
MESSENGER
Both dead, and they who live deserve to
die.
CHORUS
Who is the slayer, who the victim? speak.
MESSENGER
Haemon; his blood shed by no stranger
hand.
CHORUS
What mean ye? by his father's or his
own?
MESSENGER
His own; in anger for his father's crime.
CHORUS
O prophet, what thou spakest comes to
pass.
MESSENGER

So stands the case; now 'tis for you to act.
CHORUS
Lo! from the palace gates I see approaching
Creon's unhappy wife, Eurydice.
Comes she by chance or learning her son's fate?
[Enter EURYDICE]
EURYDICE
Ye men of Thebes, I overheard your talk.
As I passed out to offer up my prayer
To Pallas, and was drawing back the bar
To open wide the door, upon my ears
There broke a wail that told of household woe
Stricken with terror in my handmaids' arms
I fell and fainted. But repeat your tale
To one not unacquaint with misery.
MESSENGER
Dear mistress, I was there and will relate
The perfect truth, omitting not one word.
Why should we gloze and flatter, to be proved
Liars hereafter? Truth is ever best.
Well, in attendance on my liege, your lord,
I crossed the plain to its utmost margin, where
The corse of Polyneices, gnawn and mauled,
Was lying yet. We offered first a prayer
To Pluto and the goddess of cross-ways,
With contrite hearts, to deprecate their ire.
Then laved with lustral waves the mangled corse,
Laid it on fresh-lopped branches, lit a pyre,
And to his memory piled a mighty mound
Of mother earth. Then to the caverned rock,

The bridal chamber of the maid and Death,
We sped, about to enter. But a guard
Heard from that godless shrine a far shrill wail,
And ran back to our lord to tell the news.
But as he nearer drew a hollow sound
Of lamentation to the King was borne.
He groaned and uttered then this bitter plaint:
"Am I a prophet? miserable me!
Is this the saddest path I ever trod?
'Tis my son's voice that calls me. On press on,
My henchmen, haste with double speed to the tomb
Where rocks down-torn have made a gap, look in
And tell me if in truth I recognize
The voice of Haemon or am heaven-deceived."
So at the bidding of our distraught lord
We looked, and in the craven's vaulted gloom
I saw the maiden lying strangled there,
A noose of linen twined about her neck;
And hard beside her, clasping her cold form,
Her lover lay bewailing his dead bride
Death-wedded, and his father's cruelty.
When the King saw him, with a terrible groan
He moved towards him, crying, "O my son
What hast thou done? What ailed thee? What mischance
Has reft thee of thy reason? O come forth,
Come forth, my son; thy father supplicates."
But the son glared at him with tiger eyes,
Spat in his face, and then, without a word,
Drew his two-hilted sword and smote, but missed

98

His father flying backwards. Then the boy,
Wroth with himself, poor wretch, incontinent
Fell on his sword and drove it through his side
Home, but yet breathing clasped in his lax arms
The maid, her pallid cheek incarnadined
With his expiring gasps. So there they lay
Two corpses, one in death. His marriage rites
Are consummated in the halls of Death:
A witness that of ills whate'er befall
Mortals' unwisdom is the worst of all.
[Exit EURYDICE]
CHORUS
What makest thou of this? The Queen has gone
Without a word importing good or ill.
MESSENGER
I marvel too, but entertain good hope.
'Tis that she shrinks in public to lament
Her son's sad ending, and in privacy
Would with her maidens mourn a private loss.
Trust me, she is discreet and will not err.
CHORUS
I know not, but strained silence, so I deem,
Is no less ominous than excessive grief.
MESSENGER
Well, let us to the house and solve our doubts,
Whether the tumult of her heart conceals
Some fell design. It may be thou art right:
Unnatural silence signifies no good.
CHORUS
    Lo! the King himself appears.
    Evidence he with him bears
    'Gainst himself (ah me! I quake
    'Gainst a king such charge to make)

But all must own,
    The guilt is his and his alone.
CREON
(Str. 1)
    Woe for sin of minds perverse,
    Deadly fraught with mortal curse.
    Behold us slain and slayers, all akin.
    Woe for my counsel dire, conceived in sin.
        Alas, my son,
        Life scarce begun,
        Thou wast undone.
    The fault was mine, mine only, O my son!
CHORUS
Too late thou seemest to perceive the truth.
CREON
(Str. 2)
By sorrow schooled. Heavy the hand of God,
Thorny and rough the paths my feet have trod,
Humbled my pride, my pleasure turned to pain;
Poor mortals, how we labor all in vain!
[Enter SECOND MESSENGER]
SECOND MESSENGER
Sorrows are thine, my lord, and more to come,
One lying at thy feet, another yet
More grievous waits thee, when thou comest home.
CREON
What woe is lacking to my tale of woes?
SECOND MESSENGER
Thy wife, the mother of thy dead son here,
Lies stricken by a fresh inflicted blow.
CREON
(Ant. 1)
    How bottomless the pit!
        Does claim me too, O Death?
        What is this word he saith,
    This woeful messenger? Say, is it fit

To slay anew a man already slain?
    Is Death at work again,
    Stroke upon stroke, first son, then
mother slain?
CHORUS
Look for thyself. She lies for all to view.
CREON
(Ant. 2)
Alas! another added woe I see.
What more remains to crown my agony?
A minute past I clasped a lifeless son,
And now another victim Death hath won.
Unhappy mother, most unhappy son!
SECOND MESSENGER
Beside the altar on a keen-edged sword
She fell and closed her eyes in night, but
erst
She mourned for Megareus who nobly
died
Long since, then for her son; with her
last breath
She cursed thee, the slayer of her child.
CREON
(Str. 3)
    I shudder with affright
O for a two-edged sword to slay outright
    A wretch like me,
    Made one with misery.
SECOND MESSENGER
'Tis true that thou wert charged by the
dead Queen
As author of both deaths, hers and her
son's.
CREON
In what wise was her self-destruction
wrought?
SECOND MESSENGER
Hearing the loud lament above her son
With her own hand she stabbed herself
to the heart.
CREON
(Str. 4)
I am the guilty cause. I did the deed,
Thy murderer. Yea, I guilty plead.

My henchmen, lead me hence, away,
away,
A cipher, less than nothing; no delay!
CHORUS
Well said, if in disaster aught is well
His past endure demand the speediest
cure.
CREON
(Ant. 3)
    Come, Fate, a friend at need,
    Come with all speed!
    Come, my best friend,
    And speed my end!
    Away, away!
Let me not look upon another day!
CHORUS
This for the morrow; to us are present
needs
That they whom it concerns must take in
hand.
CREON
I join your prayer that echoes my desire.
CHORUS
O pray not, prayers are idle; from the
doom
Of fate for mortals refuge is there none.
CREON
(Ant. 4)
Away with me, a worthless wretch who
slew
Unwitting thee, my son, thy mother too.
Whither to turn I know now; every way
        Leads but astray,
And on my head I feel the heavy weight
        Of crushing Fate.
CHORUS
    Of happiness the chiefest part
        Is a wise heart:
    And to defraud the gods in aught
        With peril's fraught.
    Swelling words of high-flown might
    Mightily the gods do smite.
    Chastisement for errors past
    Wisdom brings to age at last.

Made in the USA
San Bernardino, CA
06 January 2019